THE CAT'S MEOW

Novels by Robert Campbell

THE CAT'S MEOW

A Jimmy Flannery Mystery

Robert Campbell

NAL BOOKS

NEW AMERICAN LIBRARY

NEW YORK AND SCARBOROUGH, ONTARIO

Copyright © 1988 by R. Wright Campbell

All rights reserved. For information address New American Library.

Published simultaneously in Canada by The New American Library of Canada Limited

NAL TRADEMARK REG. U.S. PAT. OFF. AND FOREIGN COUNTRIES
REGISTERED TRADEMARK—MARCA REGISTRADA
HECHO EN CHICAGO, U.S.A.

SIGNET, SIGNET CLASSIC, MENTOR, ONYX, PLUME, MERIDIAN and NAL BOOKS are published *in the United States* by NAL PENGUIN INC., 1633 Broadway, New York, New York 10019, *in Canada* by The New American Library of Canada Limited, 81 Mack Avenue, Scarborough, Ontario M1L 1M8

Library of Congress Cataloging-in-Publication Data

Campbell, R. Wright.
  The cat's meow.

  I. Title.
PS3553.A4867C3 1988   813'.54   88-9880
ISBN 0-453-00615-9

Designed by Leonard Telesca

First Printing, October, 1988

1 2 3 4 5 6 7 8 9

PRINTED IN THE UNITED STATES OF AMERICA

To Jane R.

1

 You might say it all starts when Father Mulrooney's cat up and dies. Its name was Ignatius. Some people called it Iggie. A few even called it Ig.

My name's James Flannery, but only my sainted mother—God keep her beside Him—ever called me that, except for my wife, Mary, who calls me James more than she calls me anything else.

Mostly people call me Jimmy and my father, Mike, calls me Jim, and there's them what call me Jimbo when they want to get my goat or put me down.

So if I'd known the priest's cat real well I probably would've called him Ignatius, or maybe Iggie or Ig but never Igo. As it turns out, I never had a chance to call him anything very often because we wasn't really friends, only passing acquaintances.

I ain't been around St. Pat's, except now and then, since I moved out of the ward over to the Twenty-seventh.

The St. Pat's I'm talking about ain't the one over on the Southeast Side, which is in South Chicago's oldest parish, having been established in 1857, although the present church and school was built in

1

1899. And it ain't the St. Pat's on the Near West Side, which they started building in 1855 but which was interrupted by a cholera epidemic so it didn't get finished until 1856 but, even so, is generally considered the oldest church in Chicago.

The St. Pat's I'm talking about is in the Fourteenth on the same block as St. Ulric's Seminary for Boys, a preparatory school of good scholastic reputation where Catholic boys are introduced to studies which could lead to the priesthood and, if not, to careers as notable Catholic laymen.

The original church was burned down around 1862 when it was only half finished, and burned down again about ten years later in the great Chicago fire. Nobody tried to rebuild it right away after that. Didn't have the heart or didn't have the money. But building was started again at the beginning of 1929. They had big ideas about gray granite and pink marble, but they got hit in the face with the market crash and the depression that followed, and ended up finishing it in red brick and poured concrete.

St. Ulric's was built about the same time. It's a three-story gray stone building that looks as much like a fort or a prison as it does like a school.

The block they're built on is two regular city blocks long, the streets coming in from the north and south midway making T intersections front and back.

So the church is on one corner and the boy's seminary on the other, with the priest's house, where Father Mulrooney has lived for nearly fifty years—I don't know how many of those cared for by the housekeeper, Mrs. Thimble—in the middle. The old churchyard and cemetery is in back and extends all the way to the next street, running the

entire length of the double block except for a patch
of backyard that belongs to the priest's house and
the school's playground, which intrudes into the
cemetery even deeper. There's a wrought-iron fence
around the cemetery with two gates in it, one by
the church and the other by St. Ulric's.

Father Mulrooney was in on the building of St.
Pat's right from the beginning. I don't mean back in
1862—though he looks frail enough to be that old
sometimes—but since 1930 when, the stories have
it, he slept at night in the shack the workmen used
for a privy during the day. He's never left, even
when they offered him chances for better churches
in richer parishes out in the suburbs. He can tell
you what every door and window cost back when it
was built and what it would be worth now if the
archdiocese ever demolished the church and sold
its parts, which he claims they're planning to do
the minute he turns his back.

Especially now when everybody, including himself, calls his church St. Pits because, for the last
ten or fifteen years, the church building, like the
parish it serves, has been going downhill, sliding
into ruin.

The word around Church circles really is that
they're waiting for St. Pits to fall down from neglect or for Father Mulrooney to die from the rav-
ages of time—whichever comes first—so they can
knock the homely pile of junk flat and either ex-
pand St. Ulric's or sell off the property where the
church stands, like they've already sold off the
churchyard. That was a couple of years ago when
the bishop decided nobody was burying there anymore, preferring more modern burial grounds scattered here and there throughout Chicago and the
suburbs. Rumor has it a gas station is going to be

put on the property. So, like Father Mulrooney often tells my father, Mike, when a man keeps hearing bullets whistling past his ear, finds deadly snakes in his bed, and his tea poisons the cat, he ain't being paranoid because he thinks somebody's out to get him.

Mike says it's time that's out to get Father Mulrooney just like it's out to get us all. The old priest is getting a little senile and sometimes, when Mike stops by for a chat or the weekly game of cards he's been having with Father Mulrooney, Rabbi Ziegler, and the Reverend Kilmonis from the First Baptist Church every Wednesday for the last twenty years, he thinks it's 1930 again and he's a young man of twenty-nine.

My old man remembers him shortly after that, back when the Fourteenth was all Irish and German with maybe a couple of Italians. Father Mulrooney, whose name is also Patrick, was tall and carried himself like a soldier. He had pale skin, ruddy cheeks, blue eyes, and black hair parted in the middle and slicked back with brilliantine until it shone like patent leather. "And a silver tongue on him," Mike says, "that soothed the men, charmed the ladies, and brought the angels down from heaven to sit among the congregation." Even though he was only a youngster at the time, going to church every Sunday and serving as altar boy as well, he remembers the gossip and the speculating about how a priest as handsome as Father Mulrooney should watch hisself or one of the bolder young women—flappers they called them—of the parish might lead him down the garden path into carnal sin.

So maybe that's why—because of old times—although he don't go to church much more than me, Mike makes the effort to do his Easter duties and drags me over to midnight Mass to see the old priest at Christmas Eve.

That's about the only time I ever see Ignatius, the old black cat. If the sacristan's forgot to fill up the big holy-water font on the wall in the vestibule just inside the front door, which is frequent, you could usually find old Ignatius curled up in the cool marble. If you pet him, he'd open one eye and turn his head so you could scratch his neck, the one fang he's got left shining like a piece of old ivory against his lip. He's what you'd call an old reprobate of a cat.

It's my father, Mike, who tells me about how Ignatius is dead. Father Mulrooney breaks the news of his bereavement at the card game a few nights before.

"I'm sorry to hear that about old Ignatius," I says. "Please give Father Mulrooney my condolences next time you play cards."

"I'm sure Father Mulrooney would like to hear your condolences from your own lips," Mike says.

I suppose my old man figures an old priest would care a hell of a lot about his cat, never having had a wife, but for some reason I always had the idea Father Mulrooney kept the cat around because he thought it suited his image of the wise old priest.

But Monday night I go over to see Father Mulrooney to say how sorry I am about his loss.

When I get there, Mrs. Thimble, his housekeeper, who looks like a mop in this house dress which is clean but very baggy, opens the door. She's as frosty as I remember her from when I was a boy when she asks me who I am in a tone of voice not supposed to make me welcome.

The only other person I know can make you feel like you never should have come before you got your foot past the door is Mrs. Banjo, Delvin's housekeeper. You'd think they were sisters except they don't look anything like one another.

"It's Jimmy Flannery, Mrs. Thimble," I says.

"Oh, the choirboy," she says.

"Well, it's been a little while since I sang in the choir."

"That's all right, since we haven't got a choir anymore," she says.

Then a voice as thin and rusty as Mrs. Thimble's says, "And it's been a long time since you've been to church at all, at all."

It's Father Mulrooney, doing his Barry Fitzgerald imitation, who was, in case you're too young to remember, an actor who did a movie called *Going My Way* with Bing Crosby some years ago.

He's standing there in the gloomy hallway, the light from the parlor spilling out all over his white hair so it looks like the shredded pages of some old book. He's not so tall anymore, the years having bent him over and shrunk him somewhat. But his eyes, even in the dim light, are still as blue as they ever were and seem to shine with a light that comes from inside his head.

"Come in, Jimmy, and sit you down," he says.

"I just stopped by to say I'm sorry about old Ignatius."

"Now, there's a story," he says, and waves me out of the cold, into the hall, and through the door of the living room.

"Tea, Mrs. Thimble, if you please," he says, staring her down in case she wants to make a complaint.

But she trots off without a murmur of protest.

"She's not herself since the cat passed away," Father Mulrooney says. "She was very fond of the creature. Very fond."

I go over and sit down in one of the big cracked leather chairs in front of the fireplace, which has an electric heater stuck in it, without taking off my overcoat.

"How are things down in the sewers?" Father Mulrooney asks.

"Moving along," I says, which is a little bit of Sanitation humor.

"I hear tell you were walking the lines lately."

"They needed my expertise for a little while there."

"I heard it was a punishment because you wouldn't play ball with the powers that be."

"Which powers is that, the mayor's office?"

"The Democratic party."

"The old one or the new one?"

"The old one. The only one there is as far as I'm concerned."

"They say the old machine's rusted and busted," I says.

"Even so I always considered loyalty and obedience virtues," he says.

"That's why I took it. I figure it's like when you was a kid. Your father or mother's got a grievance they expect you to make up for, you don't argue. You take what's coming to you and get on with it. Besides, me having to walk the sewers again is ancient history."

"I was going to add, I'm not so sure about unquestioning loyalty and blind obedience anymore."

He hesitates as though he's thinking about what he's just said and then he shakes hisself. "You cold?" he asks.

"I'm fine, Father," I says.

He's wearing a sweater and wool gloves with the fingers cut out. He's got a scarf around his neck and I can see his breath when he speaks, but he says, "So, why don't you take off your coat and stay awhile?"

He's really not asking, he's telling, so I stand up and take off my coat. I hand it to Father Mulrooney, who tosses it on the couch, which I could have done for myself. I sit down again in my sweater with my scarf still around my neck.

"You'll have a little something?" he asks.

"I don't indulge, Father."

"And very wise, too." He goes to a heavy side-board made of carved black wood, big enough to be a giant's coffin, and pours hisself a couple of fingers which he brings back to his chair with him. He cradles it on his stomach as he slouches down and puts his feet out until they're almost touching the electric grill.

"There's a stereotype, not quite a joke," he says, "of the drunkard priest drowning his loneliness and his withered hunger for women with whiskey. Let me tell you, there's drinkers among us but the reason is more often the fear of abandonment and poverty than frustration and solitude. Would you be amazed to know the Church does not provide?"

"Provide what, Father?" I says.

"A pension. A comfortable and dignified retirement."

"I always thought there was a home for old priests—"

"Filled up. With a waiting list as long as your arm. No, we're expected to provide for ourselves. After taking on the vow of poverty and giving away all the substance that might ever come my way, just how would that happen, will you tell me?"

I hardly know what to say. "I could ask around and see what I can do," I says. "I never dreamed."

He lets go the glass and waves both hands in the air, balancing the glass on his stomach without spilling a drop. "Don't fret yourself," he says. "I doubt they'll have the gall to throw me out into the gutter. I hope to die right here in St. Pat's just like old Ignatius. But I promise, unlike old Ignatius, I won't come back and prowl the church."

He gives me the old sidelong one-eye like all the best storytellers do, getting you on edge, raising the curtain so to speak. I know I'm about to hear some strange story about his cat.

"Was there something special about the way old Ignatius died?" I asks, priming the pump.

"Well, who's to say much about the way a cat dies?" he says. "Cats are funny creatures who live in a world and according to rules we don't know much about. It's not for nothing they're shown in pictures riding broomsticks with witches. It's not for nothing they write about cats sitting down to sup with imps. It's not for nothing a person will wake up in the night and find his cat sitting on his chest staring at him."

Most people don't know it, but priests, particularly old ones, particularly ones that came from the old country when they was almost grown, often get the old magic and the dogma of the Church all mixed up together in one bag. Saints and devils, prayers and incantations, pagan rites and Catholic ceremonies, the knocking on wood to summon a druid and crossing yourself when speaking the name of Jesus Christ—all spring out of the same old past and sometimes it's hard for them, just like it is for us, to know the difference.

"There's nothing special about the way Ignatius died," Father Mulrooney says, "if you think it's nothing special for a cat, lying by the fire and warming himself, to suddenly jump straight up and run the hell out of the room, down the hall, and out the back porch window, which we kept cracked a couple of inches for any sudden calls of nature."

"Was he a good watch cat?" I asks.

He gives me the old cockeye as if he fears I've gone mad.

"I have a friend, by the name of Willy Dink," I explain, "keeps a menagerie of exotic animals, including a dog what can whistle through its teeth, and a ferret that hunts rats inside the walls of old buildings, who depends on a cat to warn him when strangers are prowling around."

"What about the dog that whistles through his teeth? Doesn't he bark?"

"He lets the cat do it. Or meow or yowl, or whatever it is the cat does to give warning."

"Watch cat?" Father Mulrooney says. "I suppose you could say old Ignatius sensed when strangers were in the vicinity. That is whenever he chose to rouse himself. Whatever his reasons, he was out of here like someone had set fire to his tail, and a few minutes later I hear a scream fit to wake the dead. It raised the hair on the back of my neck, I can tell you. A cat, in dire distress, screams like a woman sorely bereaved or wounded, did you know? I went out looking in the garden. Then heard the scream again. It come from the church."

"You heard the scream right through the stone walls of the church?" I says.

"It was such an amazing scream," Father Mulrooney says, daring me to doubt him.

"He had a hundred ways to get inside the church, I suppose," I says.

"A cat has a hundred ways inside every place but heaven," he says. "I go in through the door to the

north porch, through the transept where the statue
of St. Patrick stands in his little shrine, and into
the crossing. I'm waiting for that hellish scream
again, you see, so I'm proceeding with caution. I
walk up to the chancel rail and through the gate up
to the steps of the presbytery, where I finally see
him."

He pauses. He takes the glass off his stomach and
has a swallow of what's in it. He knows how to spin
a yarn, how to draw out the suspense.

"There he was," Father Mulrooney goes on.
"There he was lying on his back in the middle of
the aisle with all four feet in the air."

Mrs. Thimble comes in with the tea. Before she
can swing around and close the door with her foot,
I catch a glimpse of somebody I think I know standing out in the entrance hall. He ducks back out of
my line of sight when he sees me looking at him. I
wonder what Phil the Junkman is doing visiting
Father Mulrooney this time of night. I didn't even
know he was Catholic.

Mrs. Thimble puts the tea tray down on the
coffee table, then goes over and whispers in Father
Mulrooney's ear. He puts aside his drink, sits up,
and gets to his feet with some difficulty.

"Don't grow old, Jimmy," he says.

"What about Ignatius?"

"Hold the thought," he says, and leaves the room.

I sit there drinking tea, smelling the peculiar
smell of poverty and neglect in the decaying house
that was threatening to fall down around the old
priest's ears, feeling my fingertips and toes going
numb, for about fifteen or twenty minutes.

When Father Mulrooney comes back he ignores
the tea and takes the position he had on the couch
with the tumbler of whiskey balanced on his stomach.

"Was that Phil the Junkman I see out in the hall?" I says.

"It was."

"You don't mind my asking what's a thief and a fence doing coming here this time of night? What's he doing coming here at all?"

"Where else would a sinner come when in distress but to the house of God?"

"You telling me Phil the Junkman comes here for you to hear some emergency confession?"

"More like a consultation. Philip's taking instruction in the faith."

"If Phil the Junkman converts to being legitimate, let alone Catholic, I'll put you up for sainthood for performing miracles, Father," I says.

He laughs and says, "Put me up for a pension, instead. Now, about the cat."

"He was laying on the floor of the church with all four feet in the air," I says, finding him his place.

"Dead as a doornail," he says.

"From what?"

"I didn't ask, and he couldn't say."

"Did you have somebody look him over?"

"A doctor?"

"Well, a vet."

"What for? I know a dead cat when I see one."

"So what did you do?"

"I buried him that very night over in the churchyard underneath the big willow."

"It's my understanding the old graveyard was sold off to an oil company," I says.

"You got it right. But I buried Ignatius underneath the tree all the same." He cocked his head and seemed to wink at me. "Though it seems that old cat won't rest in peace even in that hallowed ground."

"How's that?" I says.

"It's three nights later that I'm awakened in the middle of the night by Ignatius screaming."

"You heard a cat complaining?"

"I heard Ignatius. I raised that ancient cat from a kitten and knew his every mew and murmur. It was Ignatius calling me. I got up and put on my robe and slippers. I took a flashlight and went out into the back garden. I walked along the path to the side door of the church and let myself in with the key I carry with me in my pocket. I crept inside, making scarcely a sound.

"Just there in St. Patrick's shrine there's a bank of votive candles, if you remember. I didn't hear the scream again but what sounded like the echo of a scream, if you know what I mean, coming from behind me. I lit a candle for the peaceful rest of old Ignatius—some would think that a sacrilege, burning a candle for the soul of a cat, but I don't know—and when I turned away from the burning candles I swear I saw the shadow of a cat on the wall of the columbarium."

"There's more than one cat in this neighborhood and more than one who knows the way into a warm church on a cold night, I'd expect," I says.

He peers at me from under eyebrows that've grown bushy over the years, like two small hedges pasted above his eyes, and says that I'm being logical.

"I like that in a sewer inspector, a civil servant charged with the orderly movement of waste through the gut of the city and the keeping of the public welfare, but this is not a subject for logic. We're dealing with mysteries here and maybe even with witchcraft."

"Well, now, Father, you're not saying that you really believe in such things."

"Did you see *The Exorcist*?" he asks.

"It was a very scary movie," I says.

"It was a good deal more than that. You notice that Jesuit with his psychiatry and scientific explanations was all wrong?"

"It was only a movie, Father," I says.

He waves his hand at me as though the subject's closed, but adds, "If there weren't such things as demons and their possession of people and places, there'd be no ceremonies for exorcising written down and ready for use."

"There's that," I says, not wanting to get into a debate about is there demons ain't there demons right on the spot.

"Anyway," he says, "I put Ignatius to rest in hallowed ground and the old devil might not like it. Who would've thought when he was a kitten, a ball of black fluff no bigger than my fist, that Ignatius would have dealings with Satan?"

He starts to reminisce and I sit there listening to stories of the grand days when he was still in his vigor and I was singing in the choir and some cat he thinks was Ignatius was a playful kitten, the days and years all mixed up together in one ball of yarn. He keeps saying when I was an altar boy because he's mixing me up with my old man and mixing up the cats, all the years getting squashed together in his old man's mind so there's a long beginning that goes on forever and a short now and a tomorrow that may be only a minute long waiting out in the shadows.

Finally, around midnight, he dozes off, the glass still balanced on his stomach.

I get up and take the glass away. He just sleeps on. I pick up my coat and go to the door.

"You'll see yourself out, then, will you?" he suddenly says.

"I'll do that, Father," I says, and tiptoe along the hall fearing to disturb Mrs. Thimble, who I believe is long since gone to bed.

But she's wide awake and comes whispering down the stairs in her slippers, holding an old chenille robe around her, and almost beats me to the door. I open it and step out into the vestibule. Then I turn back.

"Are you a light sleeper, Mrs. Thimble?" I asks.

"A mosquito breaking wind will rouse me from a sound sleep," she says.

"You hear Ignatius screaming the night he died?"

"His death throes. They were very loud."

"And a few nights later, when Father Mulrooney got out of bed— "

"He sleeps downstairs and I sleep up."

"Even so, did you happen to hear a cat screaming that night as well?"

She looks at me carefully and finally she says, "The Father's almost ninety. Nightmares are to be expected."

"Then, you didn't hear anything?"

"I slept through the night."

I step out into the cold and she closes the door behind me.

When I get home, Mary's gone to work on the midnight-to-eight over to the hospital but my father and Alfie, my dog, are there to greet me.

After he sniffs me, Alfie gives me a doubtful look, like maybe I'm harboring a cat under my coat.

"The cat you smell on me ain't around anymore, Alfie," I says. "At least I hope it ain't."

"You want a cup of something?" my father asks.

"You stay here just to see I got home safe?" I asks.

"Mary and me got to talking and then it was time

for her to go to work and then I watched the news and then I fell asleep and then Alfie woke me up when he heard you coming and now I guess I'm ready to go home if you don't want a cup of something with me."

"I've had enough tea to keep me up and running to the toilet all night as it is. But how about you stay here tonight? We can make up the couch and talk a little before we go to sleep?" I says, because I can see he's feeling lonely and blue for some reason and besides there's things I'd like to know.

2

 "Time's a sorceress and memory plays tricks," my father says. He's sitting on the couch in his underwear with a blanket wrapped around his legs, still a vigorous and good-looking man, not very old as age is reckoned nowadays.

There was a time when a man, having reached a certain age, suddenly appeared wearing oxford shoes in brown or black that laced up, and cardigan sweaters without collars of a certain color, dull brown or green or gray. That meant he was old and people started calling him Grampa.

I think if I ever gave Mike a sweater like that he'd use it to wrap up the garbage. He likes to wear sweatsuits and running shoes and only plays he's getting old when he misses my mother—God bless her—and wants a little sympathy.

"Memory plays tricks," he says again. "Sometimes I think I was grown when I served Mass with Father Mulrooney, but I was only a boy, of course, about as old as you when you sang in the choir."

"You remember when Mrs. Thimble came to keep house for Father Mulrooney?"

"Oh, yes. But not only for Father Mulrooney. There was two other priests living in the house and serving the parish then. Father Morrison and Father Donovan. They went on to better things."

"How long ago would that be when she first came?"

He looks up at the ceiling and watches the years go by. "Forty years, I'd say. Just about forty years."

"So Father Mulrooney would've been about in his late forties?"

"That seems right."

"And Mrs. Thimble? How old was she?"

"Twenty-two or -three, maybe. She was a plain woman, I seem to remember, but what do boys know about such things?"

"Plain or pretty, what was she doing burying herself away being the housekeeper for a bunch of priests?"

"I don't know. She was originally from some big city in the East. New York or Boston maybe. Married a farmer from Indiana. He was killed in the war, I seem to remember somebody saying. She had no family and not much money. Gave up the farm and came to Chicago to start her life over."

"There must've been plenty of jobs around if the war was still on."

"I suppose there were. This could've been just after when jobs started getting scarce. Or maybe she just came to church looking for some comfort and someplace along the line they offered her a job. Maybe she didn't plan on staying but the years just went by. They do that. They go by and you don't notice."

"Even so, you say she was a young woman. She'd had a husband. She had a whole life ahead of her. You'd think she'd want to marry again. Start a family."

"Well, there's love to consider."

"How's that?"

"Maybe she didn't meet anybody she fell in love with."

"Or maybe she met somebody she fell in love with but couldn't do anything about."

"You're thinking one of the priests?"

"I'm thinking Father Mulrooney. They say he was catnip to the ladies."

Mike's quiet for a long time. "It's possible," he finally says. "There was talk at the time. In fact, the archbishop's office tried to make a change and offered Mrs. Thimble a clerk's job with them—they're not fools about such things—but Father Mulrooney wouldn't have it. And neither, I don't think, would she."

"So there was an old scandal?"

"No scandal. A few complaints maybe. But Father Mulrooney was well-loved by his congregation and Mrs. Thimble made herself scarce. There were no bastard babies. What they couldn't see they forgot about in time. The old guard moved out. The new people moving in saw an old priest and a dried-up old stick of a woman with a mop of dry hair on her head."

"I saw Phil the Junkman over at Father Mulrooney's house," I says, changing the subject. "It surprised me."

"Maybe he lives in the neighborhood. It's changed a lot since we lived there. All types have squeezed in. Gonifs, pimps, gypsies, blacks, and Latinos. All types."

I don't want to point out that he's lumping the thieves and the underprivileged in the same bag because he'd say I'm deliberately making an argument, trying to make him look like a bigot, which he ain't, when all he's doing is telling it like it is. And I'll say I understand that crime goes where the blacks and Latinos go because poverty pushes a lot of them into crime and the criminal element among them do wrong, mostly to their own, and the next thing I know he'll be scolding me for saying bad things about the people he would never say bad things about in a million years, but merely mentioned while he was explaining the social changes in a typical Chicago neighborhood. So I let it go.

"Father Mulrooney told me Phil the Junkman was taking instruction and was going to convert," I says. "It's pretty hard for me to believe that Phil the Junkman would convert anything except stolen goods into cash."

"Well, there you go thinking bad things about a person who's maybe trying to turn over a new leaf," Mike says, just like I expect him to. "You got to give a person like Phil the Junkman the benefit of the doubt. Times change and people change. The years go by, and the first thing you know a person starts thinking about the hereafter and should they maybe take out a little insurance policy. Maybe Phil the Junkman is playing it safe."

"And maybe he's looking for something to steal."

"I think it's time for us to get some sleep," Mike says.

3

The next day I get a call from my old chinaman, Chips Delvin. He sounds all upset but won't tell me what's bothering him. He says he wants to tell me what it's all about in person. So I grab my coat and hat and walk over to the El, where I get the train which takes me to the neighborhood where he's lived all these years, while the faces in it change all around him.

I go to his house with the lace curtains in the front windows and ring the doorbell. Mrs. Banjo makes me stand there a long time, feeling the cold creeping up my legs and the wind from the lake slipping down the collar of my coat in spite of the scarf which I've got wrapped around me twice.

"Why aren't you wearing your galoshes?" she says to me the minute she opens the door. "Can't you see it's going to snow?"

"Mr. Delvin sounded in such a hurry, I didn't stop to think."

"That's how people take sick and die from wet feet," she says, always cheerful and full of information.

21

She leaves me standing in the hall looking at the
fading family pictures like she always does while she
goes in to see if Delvin can receive me, putting aside
altogether the fact that I wasn't arriving uninvited.

I almost faint when the old man hisself comes
lumbering out into the hallway from the parlor in
his slippers. It's not like him to honor anybody that
way, especially me, since he's always thinking of
ways to keep me humble, never letting me forget
that he was the one who got me my first job in
Sewers and set me on the road to success in my
political career. Such as it is.

There was a time, I think, when he dreamed of
passing on the mantle to me like I was his son,
having no son of his own. But now a lot of people
say the Democratic party machine has fallen all to
pieces. The incumbent mayor has consolidated his
first election with a considerable increase in the
number of aldermen on his side, a beautiful Latino
lipstick lesbian by the name of Janet Canarias has
taken the alderman's seat away from Delvin in the
Twenty-seventh, Democrats are turning Republi-
can and running against incumbents, and things
are generally not looking favorable for my old
chinaman—which is what you'd say is like a political mentor—to ever gain power again.

He's still the committeeman in the Twenty-
seventh but passing that on to me would be like
passing on a quart of sour milk. In other words,
times has changed like they always have and always will and Delvin wasn't quick enough leaving
the ball before they started turning out the lights.

He comes at me with his head swinging from side
to side, his eyes weeping like the eyes of an old
elephant, and his hand stretched out to me ready to
beg a favor and my sympathy.

He throws a heavy arm around my shoulders and drags my coat off me, handing it in the direction of Mrs. Banjo, but letting go before she snatches it, so it falls on the floor where she leaves it lay while she goes out to get some hot drinks. Coffee, tea, water with lemon, cocoa, or whatever. Always with a little something in it. It don't matter to me. I don't ever drink mine, so Delvin drinks it for me.

He shows me into the living room. The shades are up but the cold light of winter can hardly fight its way through the heavy lace curtains. He picks up a shawl from the seat of his favorite chair and drapes it over his shoulders before sitting down. He points with his chin and I'm given to know he wants the footstool, which he's pushed just a bit too far away when getting up to greet me, put under his feet.

I bend over and do the favor. Then I sit down and cross my legs.

"Oh, what it would be like to bend and swivel and pirouette like a young man again," he says, his voice filled with dramatic envy.

I don't know what to say to that, so I don't say anything.

"I'm getting old, Jimmy," he says.

I don't know what to say to that either, but I can't just sit there saying nothing, so I says, "Not as old as some."

"Who did you have in mind?"

"Well, Dunleavy for one. Father Mulrooney for another."

"I sometimes think you have the gift of prophecy," he says, "the way you pluck names and things out of the air which are the very names and things which are on my mind."

"Father Mulrooney and Wally Dunleavy are on your mind?"

"Father Mulrooney is much in my thoughts. I've been thinking of the old father and the cemetery behind St. Pat's where my family's buried."

"I thought I went to your mother's funeral over to St. Mary's?"

"My mother and father are buried there. But my grandparents on my mother's side and others are buried over in the old churchyard in back of St. Pat's."

"Nobody's been buried there for years. In fact, it's my understanding that it was sold off to a gasoline company not long ago," I says.

"That one slipped by me, I'm sad to say. The cemetery's in the Fourteenth, after all, and I don't always get the news from the other wards of the city like I used to."

"I never knew that to happen before," I says.

"It's just started now that I'm growing old," he says. "It's what this gasoline company intends to do next what finally knocks me out of bed."

"What's that?"

"They're going to start digging up people near and dear to me and put a service station on the spot. My grandmother, Roseann, on my mother's side, and her fifth husband, Sean Michael. Also her second husband, Patrick, and the fourth, Aloysius. Plus her sister, Molly, her husband, Jack, and two of her three kids. And my great-grandmother, Wilda, besides. All buried out there in the Fourteenth. Wilda started it all. St. Patrick's was her church and the churchyard her last bedroom she always said. That's what I was told. Are you a religious man, Jimmy?"

"I don't know about religious. I used to be a

choirboy, but that was years ago. I go to midnight Mass at Christmas but I haven't been to confession in fifteen years. I suppose I'm what some might call a lost sheep."

"You're looking at another. You know how it is? It's the women keep us in good with the Lord. The men give up the Church soon enough and don't return to it until they feel the cold hand reaching out to snatch them away."

I wonder if he's been tapping the whiskey decanter unbeknownst to Mrs. Banjo, who, though she allows him his little toddy when visitors like myself come to call, and even winks an eye at the double he manages for hisself with teetotalers like myself, don't otherwise allow much drinking around the house. It's a well-known fact that Irishmen get maudlin with the drink in them, weeping about lost love and the cruel specter of death waiting for them just around the next turning of the lane.

On the other hand, Delvin is one of the best actors in Chicago politics and he's probably just oiling me up for a big favor.

He wipes his runny eyes with a big handkerchief he gets from the back pocket of his trousers, and blows his nose.

"Now this situation has developed in the Fourteenth and my ward is the Twenty-seventh," he says. "You'd think the committeeman from one ward could go ask the favor of a committeeman of another ward, but the Fourteenth, once in the hands of my old pal, George Lurgan, has slipped out of the control of the true democratic organization and now is in the hands of one of the mayor's men."

"Mrs. Hilda Moskowitz."

"Who will not give me the time of day."

"If she won't give you the time of day, what makes you think she'll give me the time of day?"

"Because in certain minds—not in mine—there's the suspicion that you're a turncoat, having refused the opportunity to take my place here in the Twenty-seventh as alderman, preferring to endorse a foreign woman who has an unnatural appetite for persons of her own persuasion."

I don't bother to point out that Janet Canarias was born and raised right here in Chicago. I don't defend her right to give her love and affection to whoever she pleases, it being nobody's business if she likes women more than she likes men. Because when somebody's got strong feelings about things like that, you can talk till you're blue in the face and it won't do no good. All it'll do is make them dig in their heels and say bad things about these people what are different just to show *you* that what you say don't influence them any—being people of such independent mind—and you lose whatever chance you ever have of making them see things different through persuasion.

I don't even remind him that the old politicians, including hisself, punished me for my defection by sending me down to walk the sewers, where I stumbled on a poor person what was chewed in half by a crocodile, which, if you don't already know about it, I haven't got time to go into at this minute.

Mrs. Banjo brings in a tray with two steaming glasses of tea and two small shots of whiskey on it just as I'm opening my mouth to raise hell about him accusing me of being a turncoat.

"Drink the whiskey and tea separate and it's good for congested lungs," she says. "Put the whiskey in the tea and sniff the steam and it'll clear up your sinuses." Then she walks out and leaves us alone again.

"You can always learn a little something about your health from Mrs. Banjo," Delvin says, batting back the shot and ignoring the tea.

"I hear this new alderman in the Fourteenth is of the same persuasion as Canarias," he goes on.

"Are you saying that Hilda Moskowitz is a lesbian?"

"I'm saying she's got a pretty dark complexion."

"Well, she's a Jewish lady, and they very often have dark skin and black hair."

"And mustaches," he says. "Levantines," Delvin adds, as though that explains it all.

"So you want me to talk to Mrs. Moskowitz and see what I can find out about the gas station and the cemetery?"

"It's the last favor I'll ever ask of you, Jimmy, my boy. The last I'll probably be able to ask of you. Are you not going to have your dram to ward off the flu?"

Before I can say yes or no he throws that one back as well.

He catches my eye, as the pleasure of it colors his face like a sunburn, and reads my mind.

"I drink too much tea as it is, Jimmy. It can do things to your plumbing when you get to be my age. All that tannic acid."

Which means that's all he's got to say to me. I get up and walk to the door.

"Did you hear about Father Mulrooney's cat?" I says.

"I heard. I've been meaning to get over there and light a candle for the poor beast, but I haven't been getting out of the house much lately. Would you do it for me, and drop a little something in the box? I'll reimburse you next time I see you. I seem to be without any change."

4

Mrs. Moskowitz is one of those ladies who marries young, helps her husband start a business, keeps a perfect house, raises three or four children, goes back to school after they're grown, and starts doing things. Like beating George Lurgan, old Eddie Lurgan's son and heir, out of his alderman's seat.

Mrs. Moskowitz and Janet Canarias are friends, though they don't always see eye to eye on matters coming before the council, Mrs. Moskowitz being a lot more conservative.

"So you're the famous Jim Flannery," she says to me the minute I walk into her office.

"I don't know how I should take that, Mrs. Moskowitz," I says.

"Take it as a compliment, Mr. Flannery."

"I'll do that if you'll call me Jimmy, Mrs. Moskowitz."

"That's okay with me. I'll call you Jimmy if you'll call me Hilda. What can I do for you, Jimmy?"

"You can tell me what you know about the disposition of a piece of property in your ward."

"Which one?"

"The cemetery behind St. Patrick's Church."

"You have people buried there?"

"No, ma'am. My mother—God rest her soul—is buried over to St. Mary's. But I have a friend who's got family going back two generations buried in it."

"I'm meeting half the old Irish Catholic families in South Chicago," she says. "It seems a good many of them have family buried in the old St. Patrick's cemetery, although it's my understanding there hasn't been a fresh interment there in thirty years."

"Well, some of these old families go back a ways."

"Be that as it may, public hearings were held at the time of the petition for the disposal of property by the diocese and nobody came forward at that time."

"When would that be?"

"I'd have to look it up. But it's been three years at least. Probably more. When one of your own was alderman of the Fourteenth."

"Well," I says, "we know it happens. People are always closing the barn door after the horse has run away."

"Be that as it may," she says again, which I think is what she says a lot, "there's nothing to be done about it now. Tell your friend to rest assured that under the laws of the state and county the remains of the departed will be disinterred with the greatest reverence and respect and will be reburied elsewhere in a cemetery of their choosing."

"I think what we have here is people not wanting the dear departed to be moved at all."

"I could push to reopen the hearings, but what we're talking about here is public apathy on the one hand and the power of an oil company on the other."

"I hope you'll be on our side if a fight develops."

"What kind of fight did you have in mind? Against the Catholic Church?"

"Well, no, against the oil company which is now the owner of a cemetery where they intend to put a gas station."

"Have you got a strategy in mind?"

"When everything else fails, a public petition sometimes gets the attention of the council."

"Since this matter's been run by the council more than once, I don't see what good a petition's going to do. Besides, I don't think the mayor would like it."

"How's that?"

"Well, figure it out for yourself, Jimmy. The Fourteenth is a poverty ward. Businesses have been moving out, not in. The gas station will mean jobs for minority youth. Also it sends the message that a big corporation isn't afraid to do business inside the Fourteenth, and the locals won't have to spend a dollar's worth of gas driving out of the Fourteenth to a neighborhood where gas prices are competitive."

I suppose she sees a look on my face, because she adds, "Things aren't very simple anymore."

"Well, if I want to try, can I use your canvassers and door-knockers?"

"Wait a minute here. This Irishman, George Lurgan, smelling defeat in the wind a couple of years before I pin him to the mat, helps the sale of a Catholic churchyard to a commercial enterprise, probably for good and sufficient under-the-table compensation, and now another Irishman, namely you, wants me to join your fight to overturn the deal your friend made."

"Just because Lurgan and me are both Irish don't mean we think alike or want the same things. It don't even necessarily mean he's my friend. But I can understand you wanting to stay in good with the mayor."

"Questioning my courage doesn't work on me. I'm not talking about kissing up, Mr. Flannery. I'm talking about making waves when there's nothing in it for me."

I give her my best smile. "Maybe it'll get you the Catholic vote, which I don't think you got in your pocket."

She smiles right back. "The Latinos are leaving the Roman Catholic Church in droves. I don't think there are enough Catholic votes I don't already have to make a difference."

"On the other hand, it wouldn't hurt to have a little insurance."

"Be that as it may, I like to provide my own insurance policies. I won't ask my campaign workers to help you. Let's be realistic, Jimmy. It's a losing cause before you even start. You must know that."

"I've been told that's my biggest problem, Mrs. Moskowitz," I says. "People are always telling me I don't know when to roll over and play dead. No pun intended."

5

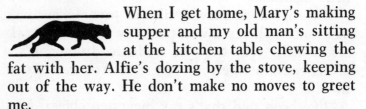 When I get home, Mary's making supper and my old man's sitting at the kitchen table chewing the fat with her. Alfie's dozing by the stove, keeping out of the way. He don't make no moves to greet me.

I give Mary a kiss on the cheek, which has got a pretty flush on it. She turns around and grabs me and says, "You can do better than that," and kisses me on the mouth. Which, in front of my father like that, makes me blush.

Mike laughs and says, "Look at him, will you? You'd think I never saw him get kissed before."

"Well, now that you're growing older and forgetful, I thought it'd embarrass you," I says, giving it right back to him.

Mary goes over and gives Mike a peck on the mouth. He turns red and grins all over his face.

"Look at you," I says.

"It's just my fair Irish complexion shows every change of my delicate emotions."

"Did you go pay your respects to Father Mulrooney about the death of his cat?" Mary says.

32

"Didn't Mike tell you?"

"Tell me what?"

"Father Mulrooney's growing old and seeing ghosts."

"Big ones or small ones?"

"The ghost of his old cat, Ignatius. Or at least he hears the cat's cry and sees its shadow on the wall."

"Was he serious or just pulling your leg?"

"He says he heard it scream at night inside the church, and when he went to have a look, the cat's shadow appeared on the wall cast by the light of the votive candles."

"I doubt the Church believes that cats have souls, so I don't see how Father Mulrooney can believe it has a ghost," Mike says.

"I told him it was probably a neighborhood cat. But he said he'd raised Ignatius from a kitten and would know his voice anywhere."

"Well, I doubt there's any danger to Father Mulrooney in it," Mary says. "He's heartsick about the death of his old cat and that's enough to give a younger person bad dreams."

I suppose she sees that I'm not totally convinced, so she takes my mind off it by asking what else I was doing during my day.

"I went over to see Delvin."

"How is the old man?"

"Thinking about the great by-and-by."

"Understandable, though I hope he doesn't begin to brood about it. Brooding shortens a man's life," Mike says.

"Maybe he should get married again," Mary says, giving my father a look which says that maybe he should be thinking about doing the same.

Ever since Mary and me get married, my father sees a lot of her mother and her mother's sister,

Sada. It seems like when he's not over to our place having supper, he's over to their place in the suburbs—Mount Pleasant, actually—where they treat him like a pasha, Charlotte buying him a pair of slippers for when they watch television together after dinner and Sada buying him a special stein for his beer.

They're as different as two women can be who were born and raised in the same family.

Charlotte's very quiet and refined, almost timid you could say, except when you look just a little closer you can see she's as tough as shoe leather and as stubborn as a ward heeler looking for an edge.

Sada's brassy and ready to argue at the drop of a hat, which, my father says, is because she was married to Emanuel Spisleman, known in political circles as Mo Spice, who was very big in the Socialist party, which is a brave thing to be in Democratic Chicago.

Mary don't usually stick her nose in other people's business but I guess every woman what ever lived is a matchmaker at heart, there being this conspiracy to get every free man married in spite of the fact that women are always saying men are lousy at being husbands.

I don't know which of these ladies, Mary's whole family, she wants my father to marry most, but she figures he's a good man and whichever one he chooses she herself will come out a winner.

The way Mary's giving Mike the eye and the little grin, I get the idea Charlotte and Sada have been talking about the possibility to her and she knows something I don't know. Maybe something which even my old man don't know he knows yet.

Women, I think, are that way—planning their

men's lives—but I don't want to have a fight about
it.

While I'm thinking about it, Mike says, "What
else did your old chinaman have to say?"

I tell him about St. Patrick's cemetery and how it
was sold while George Lurgan was alderman and
how Delvin is concerned about the removal of his
ancestors to some other place and how I went and
spoke to Mrs. Moskowitz about it and how she said
there wasn't much she could do about it, not even
let me use her campaign workers to knock on doors
for a petition.

"I wonder if she'd have any suggestions if it
happened to be a Jewish cemetery they were about
to desecrate?" Mike says.

"Well, maybe she'd dig into it a little harder,
that's only understandable," I says. "People always
work harder for things that are closer to them."

"There you have it in a nutshell. This Moskowitz
is supposed to be a servant of the people, but she
don't much give a damn if it's Catholics being
pushed around."

"I don't think that's the way it is with Mrs.
Moskowitz," I says. "After all, it's the Catholic
Church itself what sold off the cemetery property."

"So, why are you criticizing Mrs. Moskowitz,
then? Wasn't it George Lurgan who should have
prevented the sale?"

He's doing it to me again. My father's got this
way of saying something not so kind about a person
or a group, and when I point out he's being bigoted,
he turns it around so it looks like I'm the one being
uncharitable and he's the one who's acting like a
saint.

"You really should be more forgiving, Jimmy," he
says. "After all, we're all God's children."

I'm about to make my protest at the way he manipulates conversations to his benefit, when I notice Mary is setting the kitchen table for four.

"Somebody coming over for supper?" I ask.

"Janet Canarias is having dinner with us. We haven't seen her for a while," Mary says.

"That's good," Mike says. "Jimmy can ask her for a little advice about this cemetery thing."

Right that second the doorbell rings and Mike says, "Well, don't keep the lady waiting, son."

I'm always glad to see Janet Canarias, who's the lipstick lesbian I told you about who beat the candidate the Democratic party puts up against her when I decline to run, and wins the alderman's seat in the Twenty-seventh.

She gives me a hug and a kiss on the cheek and says very loud, "Wipe that lipstick off before Mary sees it," making a joke about how we're carrying on behind everybody's back and how, like she says, she'd change her luck if I weren't married.

When we go into the kitchen she hugs Mary and gives my old man a smacker, which he enjoys even though he's got his doubts about people who love people of the same sex.

After supper I tell the story about the church-yard still another time.

"I'd have to look it up," she says, "but I think I remember a little about the law that covers such things. First of all, the law doesn't lightly sanction disinterment and reinterment and will try to resolve any differences between the deceased, the survivors, the public, and the laws of eminent domain that arise from such a circumstance. Second, between the interests of the dead and the interests of the living, those of the living prevail. Third, since few such cases are open to pat solutions, each one is heard and decided on its own merits and are settled with as much sensitivity to religious, national, and ethnic considerations as possible. Fourth, in the matter of the discovery of burial grounds with archaeological significance, sufficient time must be allowed for proper evaluation of the site. You might check with Streets and Parks to see if there's the possibility of the ground having historical significance."

"Like what?"

"Like if there's somebody famous buried there."

"I doubt that," I says. "But it's very old."

"I don't think that'll be enough. Maybe if you dig around—no pun intended—you'll come up with something."

I get a feeling that there's going to be a lot of that no-pun-intended stuff, because everything you say seems to have some bearing on cemeteries when you're into something like this and everybody's going to be saying no pun intended.

"But I doubt it," she goes on. "You tell me that the diocese willingly sold the land and the threat to those interred within it is not the result of legal condemnation or municipal confiscation. So it looks to me like the archdiocese won't even lend a hand if you decide to make a fight of it by public outcry or petition. I don't see what you can do for Mr. Delvin. I'm sorry I can't be of more help."

"Thank you very much, you already helped a lot," I says. "Have another piece of Irish soda bread?"

After supper, while Mary and Janet are doing the dishes—which I volunteer Mike and me to do but they won't let us because then how could they say that men always let the women do the dishes after having guests for supper?—Mike and me go into the living room and rest our feet.

"You see much of the firemen over to the Fourteenth anymore?" I asks.

"Sure. Once a week, maybe twice, I take a drive. Tony Carlucci and Brian O'Ryan are still on the job. Carlucci says he don't want retirement. Wouldn't know what to do with it. O'Ryan says he's ready to move up to his place on Fox Lake, but Maureen don't want to move too far away from the grandkids for the whole year at a time."

"They still hear things like you used to hear things?"

"Being a fireman you can't help but hear things. The firemen know what the cops know, what the medics know, even what the morticians know. So what is it you want to know?"

"Is anybody making a business out of busting into poor boxes? Are the street people getting into the churches to stay warm now that winter's coming on? What's Phil the Junkman doing for a living now that he's found Jesus and is taking instruction in the Catholic faith? Do they ever hear of the kids over to St. Ulric's causing any trouble? What do Carlucci and O'Ryan or any of the other old-timers know about Mrs. Thimble that you don't know?"

"You sure do want to know a lot," Mike says.

"Also what do they know about the old cemetery that used to belong to St. Pat's that could help me with this problem which Delvin has tossed in my lap?"

6

The next day I take Alfie and the car and go down to see the director of Streets and Sanitation, Delvin's old crony, Wally Dunleavy, who keeps his office in the middle of a jumble of offices through which you got to make your way, knowing that calls are going ahead and files are being searched just so he can astound you with his memory when you finally get to him. It pleases him that people should think he's got all these facts in his head just like he's got this map of the city in his head so he can find any alley, any building, in the time it takes you to blink.

"Mike Flannery's kid, isn't it?" he says after I knock on the door and he says come in.

"Yes, sir," I says.

"Still with Sewers, are you?"

"Yes, sir."

"Not getting into any more trouble with any beasts, are you? It seems to me I remember you're forever getting into trouble with gorillas, alligators, dogs, rats, and the like."

"I've had a few encounters," I says.

39

"Throw those plat books on the floor and have a seat," he says.

I take the pile off the chair and lay them on another pile on the floor. There's hardly a square foot of empty space on any flat surface in the room. His desk is covered with opened maps and he's working on one with red ink and a ruler, deciding how Chicago is going to look someday if he has anything to say about it.

"What can I do you for?" he says, saying the old formula like it was new.

"I want to ask a favor for a friend."

"Who's your friend? Nobody queer?"

"You'll have to decide about that, Mr. Dunleavy, since it's on behalf of a friend of yours that I'm asking the favor. I'm just sort of like a messenger."

"Don't keep me in suspense, Jimmy. Who're we talking about?"

"Chips Delvin. I've come to make some inquiries about old St. Pat's cemetery on his behalf."

"Not passed away, is he?"

"No, sir."

"For a second there you gave me a start," he says, hardly able to hide the smile what almost popped up there when he thought he'd outlasted another of his generation.

"It's come to Mr. Delvin's attention that the cemetery where some of his family's buried is about to be dug up and turned into a gas station."

"Hold that thought," Dunleavy says as he starts pawing through the mess of maps and documents on his desk. He plucks out a sheet of paper like it's one plum out of a peck, then roots around some more until he comes up with another sheet of paper which he gives a quick once-over through the top half of his specs. Then he's up on his feet and over to the green filing cabinets which occupy more than half the floor space, opening one drawer after another and pulling out folders until he's got half a dozen of them under his arm.

"It's all here," he says. "Copy of the original deed, the bill of sale, petition to the planning commission, notification to the gas and electric company, the phone company, water company—everybody's got to be informed when there's some heavy digging going to start—request for cooperation from police, fire, and from my own department. Also maps going back to the turn of the century."

He's loving it. Here's the payoff for all his years of devotion to the streets of Chicago. Here's his chance to show off how he knows every intersection, gas pipe, and water main. Here's his chance to show me that what I know about the sewer system wouldn't fill a flea's eye compared to what he has to know about the whole shebang.

"Here's an old map shows Fort Dearborn back in 1804. During the Indian War of Tecumseh, chief of the Shawnee, the garrison escaped the fort but were attacked in a place a couple of miles away known to the Indians as *she-kag-ong*, 'wild onion place.' The fort was reestablished and occupied now and then till it was finally abandoned altogether around 1837. This map's from 1845. Take a look. See? There's no church and no churchyard on it. During the Civil War it looks, according to this map here, that a large camp for Confederate prisoners of war was located on and around it."

"Any of them buried there?"

"That could be, that could very well be, but there's no record of any that I know about." He shuffled the maps and unrolled another. "In 1871 the original church buildings were burnt down along with half the town when Mrs. O'Leary's cow kicked over the lantern."

"It burned down once before that," I says.

"Who told you that?"

"I don't know. Maybe Father Mulrooney told me when I was a choirboy years ago."

"Well, maybe," he says, tending to doubt anything he ain't got a paper or a map to prove. "This next map was done for the survey of 1903. There's the site of St. Pat's but no church building yet, and there's the neighborhood, mostly residential."

He starts to unroll another map, but thinks better of it. Maybe he decides he ain't going to waste all this learning on somebody who plainly thinks he knows more than the teacher. He cuts out forty years and shows me a map made for the Chicago Land Clearance Commission in 1947.

"Look at this. Industry moving in. Neighborhood falling apart all around the church."

"It wasn't falling apart," I says. "My mother and father was living there."

"It wasn't falling apart all over maybe, but it was falling apart. Take my word for it. See this overlay? Ten years later. And this one? Ten years after that. I started making these overlays right after I come to work here. See this gray? That's urban decay creeping up."

I put my finger on the map, marking the intersection of the streets where I was born and raised.

Each tissue overlay shows the neighborhood falling apart just like Dunleavy's saying it did.

"Hey, you could hardly notice it if you was living there. It's like growing old. First you break a tooth and the one next to it falls out. Then you sprain your thumb and it don't heal right away. Then you cut yourself and the same thing. Then one day you hurt like hell getting out of bed and you look in the mirror and you say to yourself, 'Jesus, Mary, and Joseph,' you say, 'when did it happen? When did I grow old? I never saw it coming. I never saw it.' "

For a minute there he's quiet, wondering why he never saw it.

"Thank you for showing me all this, Mr. Dunleavy," I says.

"What's that?"

"Thanks for showing me the maps."

"Well, I'm showing you the maps, Jimmy, because I wanted you to understand the land the Church sold off don't come under any zoning or restrictions that says it can't be used for a gas station. Look at all them main thoroughfares converging right there. Look at all them roads," he says like he loved all them lines and roads and boundaries of a city that was always changing.

7

 I got some flow meters to check over to the first district on South Peoria. While I'm driving I have a little chat with Alfie, who's a very good listener.

"You don't worry about where you're going to be planted, do you, Alfie?" I says.

He gives me a look like what do I know about what a dog worries about.

"Don't get me wrong. I'll find you a nice spot. Maybe out in the backyard under the tree."

He clears his throat like he don't like to point out the backyard ain't very pretty and the tree ain't very big.

So I check the meters, which takes me maybe two hours, what with the fact that I chew the fat with a couple of the engineers, and then Alfie and me drive home.

When we get there he gets out of the car fast. I open the hall door and he runs up the stairs without waiting for me. Maybe he's still thinking about what I said about burying him someday. They say that dogs got short memories and don't really think, which may be true, but I've got an idea they get into moods just like you or me.

The house is empty. I call Mary's name and I get nothing back. Then I remember this is the night she does her once-every-two-weeks double shift, four in the evening until eight the next morning. My father's not there for supper either, which he tries not to be on the nights when I do the cooking, preferring the food and attention he gets over to Charlotte's and Aunt Sada's. That leaves Alfie and me all on our own.

I give Alfie some soup in his bowl. Then I put mine back on the stove to get a little hotter.

I sit there having my soup and a heel of the Irish soda bread, thinking about how lonely I must've been but didn't know it when I used to come in off the streets into an apartment with nobody in it. Or maybe I wasn't really lonely. Maybe you only get to feeling lonely after you have somebody to live with for a while and you come home and they're not there.

I'm thinking that maybe if we have a baby, Mary'll quit her job over to Passavant, which is very hard and can burn a person out, and she could stay home and I'd never come back to a lonely house again.

That's me making up her mind for her. I already know that Mary figures if we have a baby it's got to be fifty-fifty. She might quit the hospital but she sure wouldn't want to quit working altogether. At least she don't think she would.

Somebody starts knocking on the kitchen door, which could only be my father, since everybody else I know uses the front.

"Is that you, Pa?" I says before I take the chain off and open up.

"It's me and Carlucci and O'Ryan. Are you going to let us freeze to death out here?"

They come in, three big men what practically fill up the kitchen. We shake hands all around.

"Long time no see," Carlucci says.

"Likewise," O'Ryan says. "You ain't growed much since I seen you last, have you?"

"Well, it's been maybe ten years, Mr. O'Ryan, and I've grown some. Take off your coats and sit down awhile."

"Not interrupting anything, are we?" Carlucci says.

"Not disturbing your peace and quiet?" O'Ryan says.

"I was just sitting here having my supper and feeling lonesome. You want some soup and bread?"

"Don't mind if we do," they says.

"What's for dessert?" my father says.

"Canned peaches is all I got."

"That's good enough for me," Carlucci says.

"You got any sweetened condensed milk?" O'Ryan asks.

I tell him that we keep it around and he grins and says, "Just like old times at the station, huh, Mike?"

I serve them out the soup and put some more in my bowl, which just about finishes the pot. I slice some more bread and get out another stick of butter.

It makes me feel good to see how easy these big men are with one another and with me. It's something I don't get a lot of, working mostly by myself the way I do, and I understand how soldiers and cops and firemen must feel about the other soldiers, cops, and firemen they trust with their lives.

"So your old man tells us you got to work up a petition and the alderman in the Fourteenth won't give you a hand and the archbishop wouldn't want the Knights or the ladies of the Sodality knocking on doors," Carlucci says.

"Which leaves your friends and your father's friends," O'Ryan says.

"The mayor's office would probably be against it," I says, wanting them to know what's what. Being city employees, they're vulnerable to some harassment if they cross the boys and girls at city hall.

"Up the mayor's sweet patootie," Carlucci says.

"They could make it hard on you if they wanted."

"They couldn't make it hard on us. They hurt one of us and they could have a general service strike that'd close up shop. Some goddamn cow kicks over a lantern and it'd be eighteen seventy-one all over again."

It seems like every citizen of Chicago knows that date.

"I appreciate the offer," I says, "but maybe we should wait until I have a talk with the archbishop."

"Say hello to the dear man for me," O'Ryan says. "Now, can we share the peaches?"

We sit there eating peaches and condensed milk while they tell me what they know and what else Mike has been able to gather elsewhere about the questions I asked him about.

"It goes in rashes," Carlucci says. "Crimes go in rashes. Like you'll get more murders, rapes, and assaults in the summer."

"Also more calls for oxygen. Heart attacks. Heat-stroke. Like that," O'Ryan chimes in.

"Spring you get your con games. Your pigeon drops, your Murphys—"

"That's where a hooker lures the john up on the roof of some building where her pimp or a couple of other hookers are waiting to pick his pockets, beat him up, and steal his pants," O'Ryan says, "without they give him any nookie."

"What do you think?" Carlucci says. "You think Jimmy Flannery don't know what's the Murphy game? You think he was born and raised in Evanston, where they pull in the streets at night?"

O'Ryan pays him no attention. "Also in spring firemen get more calls for fires in empty lots. The kids like to roast mickeys—"

"Potatoes," Carlucci says.

"Talk about dumb. You think an Irish kid like Jimmy here don't know what's a mickey? He knows what's a mickey better'n a guinea like you."

Carlucci grins and tells O'Ryan to shut his mouth. "Anyway, the kids start these fires in the dry weeds in the spring."

"Also in the fall," O'Ryan says.

"What about robbing poor boxes in the Fourteenth?" Mike says.

"We was going to say. In the winter we get fires in abandoned buildings where derelicts and vagrants go to try and get warm. They go into churches or try to sleep in church doorways. Sometimes they build fires to warm themselves."

"And sometimes I think they burn the church doors because they're so mad the churches ain't doing what they think they should be doing to help them."

"Anyway, sometimes they manage to get inside the church and break open the poor boxes."

"In which there usually ain't a dime because they get cleaned out by somebody working in the church every night."

"They have to break into the churches," Carlucci says, like he feels that's an awful shame.

"Even when they break in, they can't get past the narthex—"

"That's the big vestibule just inside the main door."

"What's the matter with you? You think a good Catholic boy like Jimmy, sang in the choir, don't know what's the narthex?"

"Well, I didn't know what was the narthex until just last year when my wife's cousin, the nun, told me what it was. So maybe Jimmy don't know what's a narthex either. Anyway, they can't get into the main church and have a lay-down in the pews because there's steel scissor gates blocking them."

"So the street people are getting into the churches sometimes but not getting very far," my old man says, "and they're busting into the poor boxes but not getting anything because they're empty."

"How about Phil the Junkman?"

"The word is that he found religion," Carlucci says, taking out some cigarette papers and a can of Prince Albert.

"The other word going around is that he's a liar and is working some kind of con on old Father Mulrooney, who could be eager to run up a last inning score of souls saved before he's called up before—"

"Don't say it!" yells Carlucci.

"—the umpire in the big ballgame in the sky."

"He said it. For God's sake, he said it." He rolls hisself a cigarette and offers the makings around but nobody wants to join him in a handmade smoke.

"Is he still fencing stuff behind his candy store?" I asks.

"Car radios, televisions, batteries, tape decks. The same old stuff. Nothing sensational. Nothing big."

"Just an accommodation for the neighborhood kids

who wouldn't have no way of earning candy money otherwise," O'Ryan says wryly.

"What do you hear about the kids over to St. Ulric's?"

"I got a nephew goes to St. Ulric's," O'Ryan says. "What's to say? They're kids. I don't see they get into any more trouble than usual. Different maybe. They smoke pot instead of sneaking cigarettes like we used to do. Nothing hard I know about. The cops ain't mad at any particular kids over to St. Ulric's."

Carlucci lights his cigarette and half of it disappears on the first drag.

"Why the hell don't you give those things up?" O'Ryan says.

"I like the horse races."

I don't know what smoking handmades has to do with horse races, but before I can ask O'Ryan speaks up.

"For a buck?" he says.

"Sure," Carlucci says.

"You in, Mike?"

My father takes a buck out of his pocket and lays it on the table.

"How about you, Jimmy?" Carlucci says, opening up the pack of papers and pulling out a sheet which has got some writing or something on it. "You in for a dollar?"

"Sure, I'm in for a dollar," I says, putting my dollar up on the table too, "but would you mind telling me what the dollar's for?"

"Horse race," Carlucci says, and he hands me the sheet of cigarette paper with six little horses and jockeys printed on one side and a finish line on the other.

"I remember them," I says. "I used to get them

from Uncle Pete when he rolled his own. I didn't think they even made them anymore."

Mike gets a clean plate and Carlucci lays the thin piece of paper with the horses printed on it faceup.

"Pick your ponies," he says.

Mike takes number one, Carlucci three, O'Ryan five and me six. Which leaves two and four.

"Anybody want to buy two horses?" Carlucci says.

"You and me, Jim, on number four, half a buck apiece?" my father says.

"Okay, it's you and me on number two, O'Ryan," Carlucci says. "Gambling makes strange bedfellows."

Then he touches this dot at the starting line with the tip of his cigarette and the six slow-burning tracks move away from each horse, eating up the paper little by little, one horse getting out ahead, then another track catching up and passing just before the finish. It's number four, so me and Mike pick up three bucks apiece off the table.

I saved the questions about Mrs. Thimble and Father Mulrooney till last.

When I ask the firemen if they remember hearing things about the priest and his housekeeper when they was kids, or did they hear any stories about them later on, they act embarrassed, as though it ain't right to be thinking such things about a priest.

"You hear things," O'Ryan says. "People like to wonder about such things. Especially nowadays, with priests and nuns leaving the Church and getting married to one another. Especially with priests coming out of the closet and saying they're queer and—"

"Gay," Carlucci says. "They don't call it queer anymore."

"Well, whatever," O'Ryan says. "My wife's cousin,

the nun, says it's very rare nowadays for a priest to be living alone with a housekeeper like Father Mulrooney and Mrs. Thimble. But, after all, they're well on in years and I think everybody should be past worrying about things like that."

"But they weren't always well on in years when they was living alone together," I says.

"That's true, but I wouldn't know," O'Ryan says, and Carlucci sits there nodding his head.

"All I remember, and I don't remember it very good," O'Ryan says, "is that there was always a lot of talk about what made Mrs. Thimble leave the town she was living in."

"Her husband was killed in the war," I says.

"Was it that?" O'Ryan says doubtfully. "I don't think it was that. What's on your mind anyway?"

"I was just wondering," I says.

The three of them leave together, after telling me again that they're ready to walk a petition for me if I want them to, and I eat the rest of the peaches and soda bread before I go into the living room and turn on the television.

8

 When the phone rings I realize that I've been looking at the screen without even seeing it.

"Is this Jimmy Flannery?" a woman's voice asks.

"It is, and who may I be speaking with?"

"Mrs. Thimble."

"Nothing wrong with the good father, I hope?"

"He's not sick, but he's not well."

"Would you run that train by me one more time, Mrs. Thimble? I think I missed a station."

"I think you'd better come over and see for yourself."

I look at the clock on the wall and I see that I wasn't just fogging off in front of the television, I'd been asleep.

"It's after midnight, Mrs. Thimble."

"If it wasn't, I wouldn't be calling," she says. "Come right away."

I leave a note for Mary and tell Alfie I can't take him with me because I don't want the apartment to be empty when she comes home. The wind comes kicking in off the lake, up the streets, through the alleys, rattling my teeth. I jump into the car and it won't turn over. I keep grinding the starter until the battery gives up. Now I got to take the El if it's still running—and maybe wait fifteen minutes on a windy platform. So I go back upstairs and call for a cab, an extravagance I don't usually allow myself, but I figure it's in a holy cause, by way of speaking.

It takes twenty minutes for the cab to arrive and another twenty over to Father Mulrooney's.

Mrs. Thimble must've been listening for my footstep on the porch or heard the slam of the taxi door, because she's waiting for me with the door open when I reach the top of the steps.

"In the parlor," she says, waving me on but not coming herself.

I open the heavy oak door and step into the room I'd been in the day before. It's like a hothouse. I see the electric fire on the hearth is blazing away but I can't believe that it's enough to make the room as hot as it is.

Father Mulrooney's laying on the old leather couch with a rug over his feet and legs, his head on a bed pillow. He opens his eyes when I get close to him.

"I told her not to call anybody," he says.

"What's the matter?"

There's a whoosh and the china in the cabinets and on the mantel rattles.

"She even lit the furnace," he says. "The old thing could easily explode and send us all to kingdom come."

"Is there a thermostat?"

"Beside the curtain pull over by the windows, but I don't have a great deal of faith in it."

I go over and find the thermostat, a very old affair, and turn it down. I have to get it all the way to off before the switch kicks in and the furnace shuts down.

"You should get that fixed," I says. "It's either off or on and nothing in between."

"A little bit like faith, wouldn't you say?"

I go over, pull a footstool close to the couch and sit down so I can look into Father Mulrooney's face while I'm talking to him. "Are you all right, Father?"

"I've had a fright."

"Not the shadow of that cat?"

"The cat was part of it."

"You heard Ignatius crying again?"

"I did. It woke me up and I went looking for the source. The cries led me into the church just like they did the other night."

"And you saw the shadow of the cat?" I says, feeling like we're talking about some horror flick showing down at the Saturday matinee.

"I saw Ignatius' corpse in St. Patrick's chapel. There was a black cross standing upside down on the altar and a pentagram traced in blood on the marble floor in front of it."

"I don't know much about these things, Father, but are you telling me somebody dug up the cat's corpse and used it in a Black Mass?"

"I'd say that was a possibility."

"Forgive me for asking, Father, but you don't really believe you've got some devil worshipers and anti-Christs living in the neighborhood?"

He looks at me like I'm the one who should have my head examined. "You're treating me like I'm senile or stupid, James, and that's foolish of you. The devil's real. The Church in all her teachings says so. You can meddle with that if you want and carry on about metaphor and symbol, but the truth is the devil's out there and there are those who worship him.

"But let's suppose, for the sake of your argument,

that there's no such thing as the devil. If somebody believes there is and means to serve him, it's as good as true, because these benighted folks'll be out there praising him and doing his dirty work.

"One way or the other there was the blood of sacrifice inscribing a pentagram on the floor of the chapel and the corpse of a black cat on the altar itself before a black wooden cross turned upside down."

"Have you called the police?"

"I have not. They'll only tell me it's somebody's rude joke, the work of vandals impossible to find."

"Have you informed the offices of the diocese?"

"After midnight? Are you daft?"

"Do you feel up to showing me?" I says.

He throws the rug off his legs and gets up with a bit of an effort, holding my arm with one hand and clutching the pectoral cross around his neck with the other.

I try to get him to put on an overcoat before we go out the back door into the cold but he's suddenly in a hurry to get it over with and won't take the time to stop. But once outside, he starts to shiver. He lets me take off my own coat and put it around his shoulders. So it's me that ends up walking out of a hot room in a sweat and having it practically freeze on my bones once we get outside. It smells like snow.

The side door creaks open when I heave on it after unlocking it with the big brass key Father Mulrooney takes out of his pocket and hands to me.

"Is this the only key to the church?"

"Oh, no. There's keys to each one of the doors, front, side, and back. Seven in all, not counting the one down to the basement. They're kept locked up in the utility closet by the kitchen in the house.

When anybody wants to use the church after it's
locked up for the night, this is the door they have
to use."

"Are there other keys to this door around?"

"The spare in the closet and only one other that I
know about. That's the one Mr. González, who cleans
up the church for lack of a regular custodian, keeps
for the convenience of it."

Inside the church some of the sidelights and overhead chandeliers are on. A few candles are gutter-
ing in the draft at the feet of St. Patrick in the
little chapel on the other side.

The nave rings with our footsteps the way
I remembered it doing when my friends and me
would go running up and down the aisles and
between the pews playing hide-and-seek before
choir practice. The eternal flame, signifying the
presence of Christ is glowing, suspended above the
altar.

We walk along the wide aisle splitting the pews
on the left-hand side of the nave, then turn down
toward the chancel in front of the altar.

Father Mulrooney leans heavy on my arm as he
shuffles alongside me. It feels like a long way to
me, it must feel twice as long to him. He pauses to
genuflect and practically pulls me down so I'll do
the same. Then we go across the aisle to St. Patrick's
chapel.

"There's no cat," he says, before I can say there's
no cat.

There's no cat, there's no bloody pentagram on
the marble floor, and there's no upside-down cross.
I even get down on my knees and rub my hand over
the floor to see if maybe I can pick up something. It
feels a little damp but it's as clean as a whistle. Not
a smudge on the palm of my hand. I smell ammonia.

"There was a corpse of a cat, and a black cross upside down, a bloodstain, and a pentagram," Father Mulrooney says, but the way he says it I know he's doubting his own senses. "Mrs. Thimble saw them too."

I go up two little steps to the altar. There's some soot or ashes scattered on it, so light and fluffy that when I move my hand to touch it with my finger it skitters around. I rub some of it between my fingers and it just leaves a little mark.

"You don't think somebody could be playing a trick on you, do you, Father?" I says.

"Who'd want to do a thing like that?"

"Kids do things like that. And you got a whole building full of kids right next door."

"Would they think it was funny to give an old man a heart attack?"

"Kids don't think about things like that. I mean, they just do what they do and are sorry later if anything goes wrong."

"Well, I'd rather have children playing pranks than a bunch of devil worshipers using the church without permission."

When we get back to the house Mrs. Thimble has turned on the furnace again. It's whooshing away like a flamethrower. Father Mulrooney says good night and I see him off to his bedroom, which is downstairs in what used to be his study next to the living room.

Mrs. Thimble meets me at the door as I'm leaving.

"Father Mulrooney says he took you into the church and you saw the cat, the cross, and the bloody pentagram."

She rolls her eyes toward heaven a little, then looks at me and says, "All I saw were shadows. An old man's dreams?"

"How come Father Mulrooney sleeps in his study?" I asks.

"It's a long way up those stairs at the end of a long day," she says.

"He's been doing it for years," I says.

"That's just the point, isn't it?" she says.

"I mean that he's used to the stairs, and a little exercise, even at his age, can't do anything but good."

She don't say anything else, just stands there looking at me with her hand on the door latch, wanting me to go.

"Does the Father have anything wrong with his heart?" I asks.

"I wouldn't know. He doesn't confide in me about his health. But I wouldn't be surprised, would you?"

"You shouldn't keep it so hot in here, Mrs. Thimble," I says.

"It's that or cold," she says, "and if I have a choice, I'd rather hot."

She yanks the door open and I step out into the vestibule. The door slams behind me and she turns the latch. I go out through the outer door and a snowflake hits me on the nose. I got a feeling there ain't going to be any cabs up on the avenue, and I'm right. I got to walk ten blocks in the falling snow before I pick up a cruising taxi.

While I'm walking I'm wondering how come, if there really is some devil cult around running Black Masses, they don't celebrate it on the main altar instead of over by St. Patrick's little chapel.

9

 The next morning I got the beginning of a cold and there's three inches of snow on the ground, but I go downstairs and get Joe Pakula, the refugee what owns the grocery store on the corner, to give me a jump start with his cables and his delivery truck.

I drive out to George Lurgan's retail and wholesale meats over on South Cottage Grove. There's no butcher shop like you'd expect. You go through a door at the side and there's a counter there where you put in your order and the clerk goes and gets it out of the cooler.

Actually Lurgan would rather not bother with the retail trade and discourages anybody who don't want to buy at least a quarter of a cow or half a lamb, but it's something to do with his license that makes him have to serve retail. If his place of business was in the Fourteenth you can bet he'd have taken care of that problem years ago.

There's a flyer pinned alongside the door advertising whole pigs and lambs for barbecue. Also wild game, goat meat, and loose chitterlings.

I go inside and step up to the counter. There's nobody there or anywhere that I can see. There's one of them little bells you give a tap sitting there, so I tap it. After a couple of minutes this Latino comes hurrying out of the cooling refrigerator.

"What can I do for you?" he says. Then he sees Alfie and says, "No animals."

"I'd like to speak to George."

He points to the sign on the wall behind him on which is printed the meats what are available in big letters.

"This what we got. No bow-wows."

"George Lurgan. I want to see George Lurgan. Tell him Jimmy Flannery."

"Ahh, Mr. Lurgan," he says, and sticks up a finger telling me to wait. But before he goes he points to Alfie and says, "No live beasts."

I wait maybe five minutes and Lurgan himself appears, looking at me sideways like he thinks I'm carrying a gun or something.

I make a big show of looking at the tails of my overcoat and the floor at my feet.

"What's the matter, George?" I says. "The way you're looking at me you'd think I was here to shoot you."

"Well, why are you here, Flannery? I ain't interested in politics anymore. Also what is that dog doing in this food establishment? It ain't allowed."

"It's cold as hell, George, and I didn't want to leave him out in the car while we talked."

"Are we going to talk?"

"I was hoping."

"All right. Come on up to my offices. You can bring the mutt." He lifts up a piece of the counter and lets me through. I follow him along a corridor between the meat lockers.

"Wait a second," he says, and pops into one of them. When he comes out he's got a sausage in his hand. "What's his name?"

"Alfie."

He gives Alfie the sausage. Alfie looks at me, waiting for the word, before he takes it.

"It's okay, Alfie," I says.

"That's a good dog," Lurgan says as Alfie gently takes the sausage from his hand.

We follow Lurgan up a flight of stairs to a glass-doored office.

Alfie goes over into the corner where he can savor his treat, him always being a delicate eater and not one to gulp his food.

Lurgan sits down and waves me to a chair on the other side of his desk.

"So, all right, what is it?"

"It's about the churchyard over to St. Pat's."

"Which St. Pat's? We got three of them in this city. I'm not even counting the suburbs or Cicero."

"The St. Pat's in the Fourteenth which used to be your ward before you lost your interest in politics."

"Before I lost my council seat to that Jew broad."

"Which I suppose is one way to describe Mrs. Moskowitz, but why is it when you say it it don't sound friendly?"

"I'm not gonna argue with you, Flannery, about the way I talk or where my favor lays."

"Just before you lost the alderman's job and lost interest in politics, you stood by while the archdiocese sold the churchyard and cemetery of St. Pat's."

"So?"

"So, why did you let that happen?"

"What did you expect me to do, fight the archbishop?"

"I don't think the archbishop was personally involved with the decision to sell off that land. I
don't think the archbishop gives a rat's ass about a
little thing like that."

"So, why don't you go ask him?"

"I'm going to ask him, but when I ask him, the
archbishop is going to say he did give a rat's ass,
that he personally wanted it sold when it was sold.
That's called protecting your subordinates. That's
called saving face. That's called politics, which I
know you have lost interest in. Who'd you cut the
deal with, Monsignor Harrigan?"

"What makes you say Monsignor Harrigan?"

"Because he thinks he's a financial wizard and is
also very ambitious. He figures he's going to sit on a
big set of balanced books when his time comes to be
the archbishop."

"So, after you talk to the archbishop, you talk to
the monsignor. And while you're at it, why don't
you talk to Father Mulrooney, you could ask him
how come he didn't come forward at the time."

"I don't know that he didn't come forward."

Lurgan looks very sly. "I'm telling you he didn't.
Well, maybe that ain't exactly right. He took a couple of steps but I told him he didn't say 'May I' and
sent him back to the start."

What's he talking about? The old kid's game,
Simon Says? Is he saying that Father Mulrooney
was about to make his objections to the sale of the
cemetery when Lurgan tells him he should have
checked with Lurgan first and backed him off?
What sin had Father Mulrooney committed, that
Lurgan got wind of, that would make the priest
duck a fight? I thought of Father Mulrooney and
Mrs. Thimble living all alone in that house after
the other priests went elsewhere.

"You got no reason to talk to me," Lurgan says, knocking me out of my thoughts.

"I just was hoping that maybe there was some little something you knew about the deal which I could use to question it."

"You want me to cut my own throat?"

"You saying there was something? You saying the sale was pushed through without due process? You saying you rushed the hearings during the Christmas holidays when practically nobody goes to hearings?"

"I'm saying maybe someday I develop an interest in politics again. I don't want anybody to be able to stand up and say I change my mind about things like a hundred-dollar hooker changes her shorts. I don't want anybody to be able to say George Lurgan's wishy-washy. It's a very bad thing to be wishy-washy."

He stands up.

"On your way out get another sausage for your dog outta the locker. Take one for yourself too."

10

 I go over to St. Ulric's and park the car in the parking lot behind the school. All the best spots by the wall and the trees out of the wind are already taken, so I have to park out in the open. I wrap a blanket over the hood, which I hope will keep some of the heat in. At least enough so it won't freeze up on me again like it did the night before. I walk over to the side entrance figuring I should've come by El and left the car and Alfie home, but I was feeling like company and Alfie's good company.

When I find the office, the first thing I do is tell the pretty young woman behind the counter that I'm the Jimmy Flannery who made the appointment first thing in the morning and would it be all right if I brought my dog in because I'm afraid to leave him in the car with the motor running for the heater in case he passes out and afraid to crack the window to let him have some fresh air in case he freezes to death.

"I think it'll be all right if you keep him on a leash," she says. "You can tie him to the leg of one of those chairs against the wall and I'll keep my eye on him while you're inside talking with Mr. Perrea."

I walk back through the biting cold to get Alfie. I can't find his leash because I hardly ever need one and there's no rope or anything in the trunk, so I use my belt, hoping that my pants won't fall down and embarrass me.

When I get to the office I tie Alfie to the leg of the chair like the young woman asked me to and go inside to meet Mr. Perrea, holding one hand out to shake and hiking up my pants with the other. Already he probably thinks there's something strange about me.

He's about forty, with sandy hair, a little mustache, and light eyebrows. Right from the beginning of our conversation he looks like he's got them raised because he wants to be polite but doesn't really know what I'm there about.

"Let me see if I understand what the problem's about. Father Mulrooney's lost his cat, Ignatius?"

"Ignatius died."

"He was a very old cat. I understand that a few nights after the death of the cat and its burial in the old churchyard, Father Mulrooney thought he heard Ignatius crying?"

"He's sure of it."

"A dead cat was crying in the night. The night after that the cat cries again. Good title that."

"I beg your pardon?" I says, giving him a little bit of the snoot just for practice.

"Good title. *The Cat Cried Again*. I've been thinking about writing a mystery."

"Good luck," I says. "We got a little real-life mystery on our hands right next door. It wasn't only the cat crying last night. Father Mulrooney tells me that he saw evidence of a Black Mass when he went to investigate."

"Oh, dear," Mr. Perrea says, as if regretting the foolishness of what I just told him. "I don't think there's much mystery about an old man having nightmares or even nighttime delusions."

"I'll give you that old Father Mulrooney ain't the man he used to be, but he don't get the vapors two nights in a row and he ain't ga-ga."

"I didn't mean to offend."

"I know you didn't. I'm just pointing out that it's a bad habit to get into, assuming that just because somebody's old they're not all there. If Father Mulrooney says he saw what looks to him like a Black Mass, I'd say it's a bet somebody's pulling a joke on him. Which I, for one, don't think is very funny."

"If true, I don't think it's very funny either. I didn't hear anything about a Black Mass. Who told you about a Black Mass?"

"Father Mulrooney hisself. Where'd you hear about the cat crying?"

"Mrs. Thimble told Mrs. Jellicoe, the school's dietician, and she told Mr. Dove and he told me. But nothing about a Black Mass. Just that old Father Mulrooney had been disturbed by a crying cat during the night and was it one of ours."

"You have a lot of cats?"

"We have no cats. We don't allow cats at St. Ulric's. But cats are no respecters of rules. Neighborhood cats come around. So we don't have any cats but we have cats, if you know what I mean?"

"You hear any cats?"

"From time to time, yes. More in the summer when they're out on the prowl than in the winter when any sensible cat has found someplace warm."

"You live here at St. Ulric's?"

"I do. An apartment goes with the position of headmaster."

"Anybody else live here?"

"Mrs. Jellicoe. Her accommodations are a provision of her employment."

"Anybody else?"

"The custodian, Mr. González, lives in the basement with his wife and three little girls."

"Everybody in all night, the last few nights?"

"I was at home. I assume Mrs. Jellicoe was home as well. Mr. González and his family would have no reason to be gone."

"Do you have an night watchman?"

"There's no need of one. We have several boarding students and they might need some help or supervision during the night. In case one of them takes ill. Something like that. I'm usually here, as is Mr. González and Mrs. Jellicoe, as I've said, but we provide another responsible person who sleeps in a room just down the hall from the dormitories."

"Who is that person?"

"The members of the staff take turns, a week at a time. The duty comes around about once every six months."

"And could you tell me who was supervising the boys at night during the last week?"

He opens up a shelf in his desk and looks at a schedule he's got taped there. "Mr. Dove."

"Who's this Mr. Dove?"

"The science teacher."

"He hear any cats last night?"

"I don't know. I haven't seen him to ask him, even if I thought to ask him."

"So you're not taking this seriously, is what you're saying?"

His mouth tightens up a little. "Show me some evidence and I'll take it seriously. Have you seen any evidence?"

"I'm still looking."

"You've looked in the church?"

"I was there last night."

"Well, then, did you see any traces of a Black Mass?"

"No, but then it took me some time getting here from my place. Somebody could have cleaned it up."

"Ask Mr. González about it."

"Why should I ask him?"

"He has a contract to clean the church. We think it's right that he should earn the extra money because the church doesn't require that much, even as big as it is. I doubt he cleans the church in the middle of the night, but anything's possible. He might have cleaned up the leftovers from a Black Mass, not even knowing what it was."

"It's funny Mrs. Thimble didn't tell your dietician about what got Father Mulrooney so upset."

"Once again you'll have to ask at the source."

"And Mr. Dove didn't say anything about hearing a cat?"

"I haven't seen him yet today," he says with that patient way teachers get with people who don't pick up on things the first time around.

"How many boarding students you got at the present time?" I asks.

"Thirty-seven."

"How many day students?"

"One hundred and forty-three."

I can see I've got my job cut out for me if I decide to question all these kids.

Perrea acts like he reads my mind, because this little grin sneaks out from underneath his mustache.

"Would you like to interview Mr. González, Mr. Dove, or Mrs. Jellicoe next?"

I tell him maybe it would be polite for me to see the lady before I see the gentlemen.

He walks me to the door and even goes into the outer office to point me the way to the kitchens. When he sees Alfie he don't look pleased.

"What's that?" he asks.

"That's my dog, Alfie," I says.

"We don't allow animals or pets inside the school."

"Well," I says, "since I ain't a student here you can't expect me to know that. Is it all right I leave him here until I'm ready to leave? It's as cold as a witch's heart out there this morning."

He says okay but I can see he ain't happy about it.

So I leave Alfie and go the way he tells me until I find the kitchens.

I don't know what I expect to meet when I meet the dietician, Mrs. Jellicoe. It certainly ain't a stunner who looks like Maureen O'Hara in her prime.

11

 I wipe the crumbs of the chocolate-chip cookie Katherine Jellicoe gave me off my mouth.

"A good cookie?" she asks.

"A very good cookie," I says.

"So you didn't hear anything about the claims Father Mulrooney makes about seeing the body of a cat and a black cross on the altar and a bloody pentagram on the floor?" I says.

"Lord preserve us from such things. I heard about the wailing cat but that's all."

"Did you hear the cat yourself?"

"If I did, I wouldn't remember, now, would I? The city's full of cats screaming, fighting, and loving all night. It's the kind of sound wouldn't wake me, I don't think."

"Do you think there could be anyone using the church for a Black Mass?"

"I can't imagine how they'd even get into the church after dark. It's locked up tight unless it's Saturday and Father Mulrooney's taking confessions or it's Sunday late Mass."

"It must be used for other things. AA meetings, Ladies' Sodality, Boy's Club, things like that."

"They use the basement entrance and there's no way past the locked door at the top of the stairs that I know about. But I suppose if somebody wanted a way in they'd find it. Evil people have a talent for such things as passing through locked doors that average people don't have."

"Do you believe in such things, then?"

She smiles. "I'm a modern woman and likely to say I don't. But there's a whole childhood and a nation in my past. How do I know what I believe and what I say I believe—or don't believe? If there's somebody having them, it's a troublesome thought, isn't it?"

"Or it could just be somebody playing games."

"Or an old man's nightmares."

We stand there thinking about it.

"Try the carrot cake, Mr. Flannery," Katherine says.

I already tried the tapioca pudding with orange slices, the apple pie, the streusel buns, and the chocolate torte with raspberry jelly between the layers.

"I really shouldn't," I says.

"Probably not, but you know you want to, so why don't you go ahead and try it?"

I take a bite and it melts in my mouth. I'm feeling guilty, almost like I'm cheating on Mary. I'm always telling my wife what a great cook she is. But what I'm eating now is better than great, and if I ever told Mary about how this lady can cook, I got the feeling she'd be almost as hurt as if I said I went to bed with this blue-eyed red-haired beauty in the kitchen of the boy's seminary.

"Desserts are the secret," she says.

"The secret to what?"

"Pleasing boys. Maybe pleasing men. Give boys chicken cordon bleu, Hommard à l'Armoricaine, or beef Wellington and you might as well be giving them a hamburger on a bun. Pommes au basilic, à la Landaise, or mousseline are nothing but spuds. But serve them up a dessert that lingers on the tongue and in the memory and you've made a slave for life. I keep my romance with the boys going with new desserts."

"I can understand," I says. "You been working here long?"

"Fourteen months."

"You like it here?"

"It's an experience."

"I guess it would be, cooking for more than two hundred kids."

"I've got kitchen help."

"Even so. It seems to me with the talents you got you could be the premiere chef at some big hotel, some fancy restaurant, maybe the home of some billionaire."

"Except for my son."

"Your son? He's here at St. Ulric's?"

"St. Ulric's is one of the finest prep schools in the state. I worked it out on a piece of paper. What I could make somewhere else. How much in extra taxes. How much for an apartment or a house. How much for tuition for Kenneth. Driving him here. Driving him there. Working out a schedule. Making it work. A single parent's life can be very difficult."

"You don't mind my asking, how old is Kenneth?"

"Thirteen."

"I got to say it's hard for me to believe a woman looks like you could have a boy thirteen years old."

She smiles into my eyes with her eyes but her

mouth pretends to be serious. "I was ten when I had him," she says. "You've got the silver tongue to go with the hair."

"You've got red hair too."

"It means different things for a woman than for a man."

"Another thing I can't believe—"

"Is that my husband would've left me?"

"It's hard to see how anybody could."

Her eyes fill up. "He couldn't help it. He was killed in an accident. Hit by a drunk driver coming back from the candy store with the newspaper and a quart of ice cream."

"I'm sorry."

"You weren't to know."

"How long ago was this?"

"Eighteen months."

"And five days?"

She gives me a crooked smile and says, "Twelve days."

"You got to stop counting."

"I'd stop counting if I could stop remembering. Are you married, Mr. Flannery?"

"Yes, I am."

"Is it any wonder?"

"Now you're buttering me up like I was scone," I says. "How's your boy handling it?"

"He tries not to let it show but he's taking it very hard. Very hard."

"It must do some good having so many kids around. Like a family. Almost like a family."

The tears start fuzzing her eyes again. It's not like a family. There's nothing like a family except a family. I reach out to her because she needs hugging. She comes into my arms and lays her cheek against the tweed. Hugs are better than almost anything when a person's been a long time lonely.

There's a hell of a racket and the swinging doors to the dining hall slam open. Three kids come barreling in. They pull up short when they see two grown-ups with their arms around each other.

Two of the kids are curious and maybe a little bit amused. The kid in front don't like it.

I don't have to be told he's Katherine's kid what with the flaming red hair. But there the resemblance ends. He's too fat for a kid his age. I'd be ready to give odds he's a couch potato, sitting in watching television while the other kids are out batting the baseball around or playing soccer. I'm willing to bet money he's got a doctor's excuse says he shouldn't overexert hisself. He's got pretty good shoulders and long legs, so if he'd cut down on the eats and do twenty laps a day he'd look okay.

He's got the meanest eyes I ever seen on a boy. He don't bother squinting his eyes; they just look hard. He's looking at me wide-eyed, like he's surprised, but I know if looks could kill I'd be dead.

Katherine feels my attention is elsewhere. She lets go, backs up, and turns around, taking the towel off her shoulder and using it to wipe her eyes.

"Kenneth," she says. "What are you doing here?"

"Free period," he says. "It's free period for Hector, Walter, and me."

"Where's the rest of your class?"

"At gymnasium."

"Don't you take gymnasium?" I ask.

"He's excused," Katherine says, just like I figured.

"Hector and Walter are excused too," Kenneth says, telling me he's not the only invalid in the joint.

"Shouldn't you be in study hall?" Katherine says.

"May we have a piece of cake, Mother?" he says, trying to put her off.

"Answer my question and we'll see."

"Mr. Dove said he was going to close his eyes for a minute and expected us to keep on studying even while he wasn't watching us," Walter pipes up.

"But he fell asleep," Hector adds. "He even started to snore."

"So when we had to go use the toilets we didn't want to bother him. It looked like he was all worn out," Kenneth says.

Katherine's cheeks get rosy. I wonder if her son's telling her he knows the reason why Mr. Dove is all worn out and that she was part of the reason.

"Have we answered your question, Mother?"

I don't like a kid who calls his mother Mother all the time. It's one of the few prejudices that I got. I think there's something unnatural about it. Maybe it's okay for some kid in England to keep on calling his mother Mother but I don't think it's right over here. A kid should call his mother Ma or Mom. I don't mean Mommy. But not Mother all the time. There's something sneaky about it.

On the other hand, most mothers like to be called Mother in front of people. They think it shows good upbringing and respect.

So this little con merchant is working his mother right in front of me. Every once in a while he gives me the sidelong eye because he knows I know but there's nothing I can do about it. First because I don't know Katherine well enough to tell her that her little sonny boy's a manipulator, and second because even if I knew her for thirty years she wouldn't believe me. Or anybody else, for that matter.

"I suppose he's answered my question. What do you think, Mr. Flannery?" That's to show the kid we're not really friendly. In fact, we're hardly acquaintances.

"I think these boys should get back to study hall before Mr. Dove wakes up," I says.

"I think they have time for just a small piece of cake," she says. Then she spots their hands. "First you'll have to wash your hands. I'm not going to let you boys eat out of your fingers with hands in that condition."

She shovels them over to the sink and turns on the taps. Walter and Hector dip their fingers under the water as though they'll melt. She just stands there, knowing all the tricks, waiting for them to pick up the soap and really give their hands a scrub.

Hector and Walter give up the struggle with hardly a peep, but Kenneth hangs back, still giving me the eye, wondering what I'm there for.

"Are you going to be a teacher here?" he asks me.

"Mr. Flannery came to look into this business about Father Mulrooney's cat and what's been happening since it died."

"What's been happening?" he asks.

"Nothing for you to concern yourself about," she says. "Now wash your hands." When he don't move fast enough she laughs, grabs him by the wrist, and puts his hand in the running water. He jerks away.

"I can do it myself, Mother," he practically yells. He turns his back and only pretends to wash his hands. Then he looks at me as if he's daring me to tell his mother he defied her. Not a very likable kid, any way you look at it.

12

I like this Maxwell Dove right off the bat.

He's a chunky guy about my height—maybe he's got an inch on me—but thicker through the shoulders and the neck. He's got sandy hair so mussed up it looks like he just got out of bed and a lopsided grin that seems to say he knows what a picture he makes but, what the hell, it's the best he can do.

"Call me Max," he says. "What do you think about the goings-on next door at St. Pat's?"

"You heard about it?"

"Who hasn't heard about it?" he says. "The kids in here are like two hundred radio stations. A fly can't fart but some kid hears it and passes it on."

"What exactly is it everybody's heard about?"

"The cat crying out from the grave. Its shadow on the wall of the church."

"That's all?"

"Is there more?"

I sketch in the business about how Father Mulrooney went into the church and saw—or thought he saw—a setup for a Black Mass.

Dove frowns and wipes his face with his hand the way some people do when they're distressed.

"Something bothering you?" I says.

"It bothers me that one of two things could be possible from what you just told me: either Father Mulrooney is getting weak in the mind or there are people playing vicious jokes on him."

"Or there's a coven of devil worshipers in the Fourteenth," I says.

"Even that's possible. We've got plenty of Puerto Ricans, Filipinos, and Haitians coming in. Black Masses are a part of those cultures."

"The two hundred radio sets ain't been broadcasting anything about something like that?"

"I haven't heard anything."

"So maybe it's just as well we don't say anything about it."

"Who else knows?"

"Just you, me, Mrs. Jellicoe, and Mr. Perrea. I told them. Naturally, Father Mulrooney and Mrs. Thimble know, but I doubt the father's going to talk about it and Mrs. Thimble seems to be more concerned about cats making a racket at night than anything else."

"Maybe she doesn't believe in what Father Mulrooney says he saw. Do you?"

"I don't know," I says. "I'm like you. Whatever's going on—did he or didn't he see what he told me he saw—it's not good. What kind of a relationship does Mr. Perrea have with the boys?" I says, suddenly changing direction.

"They don't talk to him except to say yes sir, no sir."

"Not a winner with them?"

"Not a winner, not a loser, since he doesn't care

one way or another what they think of him. What are you getting at?"

"You get a teacher or a principal—"

"Headmaster?"

"What?"

"That's what Mr. Perrea calls himself, the headmaster."

"So you get a headmaster the boys maybe don't like and maybe they start thinking up ways to make his life miserable."

"Why pick on Father Mulrooney, then?"

"I don't know. I'm just poking around, seeing if one thing can lead to another. How about yourself?"

"How about me what?"

"How do you get along with the boys?"

"Oh, I like boys and I hope they like me."

"You like teaching them?"

"If I didn't I'd surely be doing something else that pays better. Yes, I like teaching."

"Science, isn't it?"

"Science and some mathematics, though Mr. Pritchard covers that subject pretty well."

"Are you short-staffed?"

"I suppose you could say that. I imagine there's not a school in the country that wouldn't say the same. If teachers had their way, there'd be no more than a dozen students to a class. If administrators and bursars had their way, the classes would be a hundred. We'd be giving lectures over closed-circuit television. In fact, some professors in big universities are already doing that."

"How many do you have on the teaching staff?"

"You'd have to ask Perrea about that. I don't bother keeping up with the roster. They come and they go."

"Can you take a guess?"

He held up a stubby hand and started ticking them off. "Miss Fichetti, languages. Mr. Ellison, English and literature. Pritchard for math I already said, and I do science. Then there's Miss Witchle for civics, and Mr. Hubbard for gymnasium."

"They still call it gymnasium?"

"No, they call it physical education, but the boys still call it gymnasium and that's what I call it."

He went on ticking off another fourteen, fifteen fingers but I don't remember half of them. I already knew if I tried to find the practical jokers in over two hundred kids, I'd have my work cut out. Now I can see if I expect to interview the entire teaching staff for clues to who those kids could be, it'd be like bailing out a pond with a spoon full of holes.

"How do you go about teaching science?" I says.

"Depends on the age of the students. Freshman you try to excite their curiosity. Mix the science with a little fun."

"Like how?"

"Like you put some baking soda and some water in a flask and plug it with a stopper. Next thing you know—pop! The kids like something like that. Then I can go on and explain the generation of gases. Or I'll soak an egg in vinegar overnight so the shell gets elastic. Toss a piece of burning paper in a soda bottle. Put the egg on the mouth. Pop! The suction pulls the egg right inside the bottle. Then I go on to explain a vacuum."

"I remember them tricks," I says. "Mr. Green was my science teacher my first year in high school and he used to do some of them things. I remember once he brought in this jar and rubbed it with a piece of wool and asked me to touch it, and when I did, a spark jumped, nearly knocked my finger off."

"Leyden jar."

"What?"

"Stores static electricity."

"I never trusted Mr. Green after that."

Dove gives a little laugh. "Well, you have to do what you have to do to get the attention of the students. Everything's show business."

"Have you got any students who're pretty quick?"

"Katherine's—Mrs. Jellicoe's boy, Kenneth—has a more-than-average interest."

"How about the two kids what hang around with him?"

"That'd be Hector Carmody and Walter Click. They have an interest, too, but they're not as keen on it as Kenneth." He gives me the eye. "You think some boys—those boys—are behind the goings-on in the church?"

"It's the kind of joke kids dream up. A little fancier than most maybe but still something a kid would think was funny."

Dove's giving it some thought. I can see he don't like the idea that some kids from St. Ulric's would be playing that kind of a joke on an old priest.

"So what do you think, Max?" I says.

"I think you think St. Ulric's has a headmaster who isn't all that popular with the students who might want to do something that could make his life uncomfortable. I think you think they could learn enough chemistry from somebody like me, who might even think it was funny, to do a few magic tricks just for the fun of it. I think you think we've got a lot of smart-alecky kids here at St. Ulric's. And you could be right. But what are you going to do about it?"

"Well, I'm going to give it some thought. In the first place, if I decide it's some practical jokers in your student body doing this, I got to warn off whoever's doing it without challenging them to do worse. I know when I was a kid, you tell me not to do this or that, I'd probably end up doing twice as much of this or that. In the second place, I got to tell Father Mulrooney about it in such a way that he gets a laugh out of it without feeling like a fool."

13

Going down to the basement by the stairs inside the building, the first thing I notice is the smell of old coal which is right in the walls even though I can see they got a big automatic furnace what burns oil now. Also there's the sharp smell of laundry bleach.

There's a room in the back which has got a line of household washers and dryers plus a couple of big commercial jobs, one of each. The smaller machines got coin slots so it looks like the boys of St. Ulric's are expected to do their own laundry.

Right next to it the basement has been partitioned off with dry wall nailed to some two-by-four framers laid on the floor. There's a sign on the door what says this is where González lives.

I knock on the door and somebody asks me in Spanish what is it?

"My name's Jimmy Flannery, Mr. González, and I'd like to ask you a few questions."

The door opens up and I almost take a step back, instinct telling me this is a very dangerous man who's staring at me.

This González is shorter than me but almost twice
as wide across. His arms are a little longer than the
average and he carries his shoulders high so it looks
like he ain't got much of a neck. But it's the face
that could pop up in your nightmares.

His skin is a dull black like the dust that's in the
walls has rubbed off on him and he's got these
blue-black tattoos on his cheeks, forehead, nose,
and chin so it looks like a vine could be crawling
over his face. His nose is so flat you got to look at
him sideways to see he's even got one. But it's the
eyes that give me the willies. They're set back in
his head so deep they're like animal eyes staring
out of jungle shadows. When he smiles it's like he
means to tear out my throat.

I tell him in what little Spanish I got that I ain't
got much Spanish and he nods his head, then steps
back with a gesture that tells me that he's asking
me in.

It looks like they partitioned out three rooms
because there's no doors in the openings, except for
one which I figure goes to the bathroom, so I can
see that there's two bedrooms besides the room I'm
already in which is like a living room and kitchen
combined.

His wife is in the corner ironing. She's tall and
light-skinned and surprisingly pretty considering
what González has got by way of good looks. She
glances at me but don't stop ironing the shirt she's
got on the board, which is only a plank set up on
the backs of two straight chairs.

González makes with the hands again telling me
I should have a seat in the overstuffed chair, which
is probably his chair and the one hospitality says he
should offer to guests. But I trump him with politeness by taking a seat on the couch, which seems to

please him because he ducks his head in a sort of a bow and takes his own chair.

I look around the walls. They're loaded with pictures of Jesus Christ, Mother Mary, and half a dozen saints suffering in one way or another. There's a big primitive painted wood crucifix and a brightly colored plaster statue of some saint, the one who got shot up with arrows, in the corner with a dozen little candles in red glass cups burning around its feet.

These ain't the usual paintings and statues you see in Catholic homes. There's a pile of skulls at the feet of one picture of Jesus and Mary sitting on a throne made of bones. There's lots of blood and corpses in the pictures of the saints too.

González's wife must've read what I was thinking because she makes a little sound halfway between a hiccup and a laugh.

González turns his head sharply, stares at her, and frowns. She don't make any more noises.

He looks back at me and does something with his face which I think means he's waiting for me to have the first word.

"Mr. Perrea tells me you're the custodian for St. Patrick's next door."

He looks at his wife again and this time it's not scolding her for being rude, it's asking for some help.

She hangs up the sparkling white shirt on a wire hanger and hooks it on a string she's got stretched in the corner. She touches her hair like women do when they're ready to enter into a social situation and says, "My husband has difficulty with English."

My mouth almost falls open because she's got this cultured voice like she was born and raised in England or educated in some English school. She

knows the impression she's made and it amuses
her. She comes over and sits on the couch next to
me, smoothing her skirt over her knees.

"My husband speaks Spanish fairly well but his
first language is Pampango."

I probably grunt in reply at first, which is how
fascinated I am with this lady and the way she
talks.

Then I remember my manners and I says, "I got
to beg your pardon but I don't know what country
it is where this Pompano is spoken." I know I ain't
pronounced it right but she don't correct me flat
out.

"Pampango," she says, hitting the *ng* a little
harder, "is the language of central Luzon in the
Philippines. My husband is an aborigine, the people
who are living in the islands thousands of years
before any others came. He is a tall man among
them."

I don't know if she means he's important back
home or what. She picks up on it right away.

"I mean that he is taller physically than the others, by a foot or more. You would be a giant among
them."

"Maybe I ought to move over there," I says, making a little joke.

"It bothers you greatly not to be as tall as other
male Americans?"

"It don't bother me greatly but there was times,
when I was a kid, when I wasn't all that happy
about it."

Her eyes flicker toward her husband. "It was the
other way around for Masbate. He was thought
gross and clumsy. Appearances, if not everything,
mean too much, don't you think?"

I can hear the sadness and the anger in her voice.

You don't have to be a social worker to know González and his wife has had their work cut out for them trying to make it in Chicago.

"You don't mind my asking, you're not an aborigine?"

"I am Tagalog. I was born and raised in Manila. My father is a doctor and my mother a professor of anthropology. Considerable accomplishments. I was training to be a linguist. That's how I met my husband. On a field study. They were not pleased when I informed them I was going to marry an abo."

"Parents can be like that. Irish Catholics want their kids to marry Irish Catholics. Okay, maybe an Italian Catholic'll do in a pinch. And Jewish people want their kids to marry Jews."

"Tribal purity was a survival tactic," she says.

"And good politics," I says. "More than Irish marrying Irish and Catholic marrying Catholic, the Democratic party in Chicago wants Democrats marrying Democrats."

She says something to Masbate, who's been sitting there looking from her to me while we're talking, but who's probably been feeling left out. He laughs out loud. It's a pretty sound, like water running over rocks.

"I told my husband your little joke about politics. He enjoys such things. Now, Mr. Flannery, what is it you want to know about my husband's employment at the church next door?"

"I'd like to know what his duties are."

She speaks to him in this language which I never heard of before and he rattles back at her.

"He's expected to check the thermostat for the furnace every day to see that no one has turned it up past fifty-eight degrees during the week."

I try to remember if the church was warm or cold when I checked it out the other night with Father Mulrooney, but I can't do it. Churches always feel colder than other places to me anyway. Maybe that's because when it's cold outside they know everybody's going to be wearing overcoats and they don't want people dropping from the heat. Maybe because it just ain't possible to heat a place with a roof that goes up thirty, forty feet without it costing a fortune.

"That's not of much concern except on Saturday after confession and Sunday after Mass when it's possible for someone to forget to turn it down. Also my husband is expected to pick up around the pews—people drop paper handkerchiefs and gum wrappers—and he sweeps and mops the floor once a week."

"Only once a week?"

"There's not much traffic in St. Patrick's. The people don't make much use of it. So it really only gets very dirty after Saturday confessions and Sunday Masses. They couldn't afford to pay him for much more than he does once a week anyway."

"What time does he clean the floors?"

"Sunday night. Actually it would be early Monday morning around one or two. My husband works long hours here at the school."

"When he does the floors, does he do the little chapel of St. Patrick's too?"

She cocks her head. "It is a special place to him."

"Does he dust the altars?"

"No, that is taken care of by the ladies of the parish. It's an honor for them."

"Does your husband ever have so much work to do that he has to let the church go till maybe later in the week?"

She speaks to him and he shakes his head, his eyes shifting to me and away like a couple of lizards looking for a rock. I don't know how to read his expression good enough to know what it means because I never seen a face like his before. It could be my question makes him afraid I'm onto something about the other night, or it could just mean he's a little insulted that anybody should think he's not doing his job right.

I ask her to ask him if he saw anything the night the cat died.

"Only the good priest burying the cat underneath the tree in the cemetery."

"How about three nights later?"

She asks him and he answers back and she says, "He says he saw nothing but he felt something in the church."

"What did he feel?"

She asks him. He answers, his eyes glinting out of these little caves in his skull.

"Restless spirits of the dead. Or the cries of a spirit anxious to fly. Or whispers from hell."

"What do you think he felt?"

She looks at me for a long while. Then she shrugs her shoulders. "I see you looking at our ikons," she says. "I can imagine how strange they are to you, all the skulls and corpses, the blood and open wounds. Our religion is deeply felt and very terrifying. My husband believes in literal matters of heaven and hell that I do not believe. Your Christ sometimes bleeds on his cross but your religion, through the years, has become a bloodless thing, I think. It is not fiercely felt or experienced. We know about the ghost of the cat and my husband believes there was something more."

"He saw something, then?"

She shakes her head. "A little thing. Some soot or ash. He believes a sacrifice may have been burned there. But it could have been the simple dirt of the city. And he felt something, something in the air. It was defiled."

"Defiled?" I says. "In what way defiled?"

"An evil ceremony took place in St. Patrick's, he believes."

Masbate said something.

"My husband says that he's afraid that a great struggle is going on for Father Mulrooney's soul."

I put my hands on my knees and lean forward, ready to stand up and leave.

She stands up before I can get to my feet. "We offered no refreshment."

"Well, I didn't come as a guest," I says.

"What did you come as, Mr. Flannery?" she says.

"Maybe I came as somebody fighting for Father Mulrooney's welfare."

Masbate stands up when I stand up and they both walk me to the door. I stick out my hand to her and she folds hers and smiles, letting me know shaking hands is not her way.

But he puts out his hand.

"Is González really your name?" I asks, wanting to show that I'm taking the effort to know them better than other people might want to know them.

She smiles at what she sees as good upbringing.

"It's the name we are known by. Our true name you would be unable to pronounce."

14

That night around eleven o'clock I tell Mary I'm going for a drive over to St. Pat's, and when she asks what for, I tell her I got an idea if I stake out Father Mulrooney's house I might catch the wise guys who're playing these cruel jokes on the old priest and giving him so many sleepless nights. She asks me how many nights I'm going to play cop sitting in a cold car, ducking down every time somebody trots by, and am I going to wear a trench coat and a snap-brim felt hat. I says that it's Friday night and the next day is Saturday when the people will be coming for confession in the morning, afternoon, and after supper at night, and the day after that is Sunday with Masses and more traffic in and out of the church so it seems to me, if anybody wants to keep this practical joke going—if it is a practical joke—this could be the night.

"If it's somebody playing jokes, they'll get tired of playing any more soon enough, especially on nights as cold as this. If you have to be on the spot, why not sit down in Father Mulrooney's parlor, where at least you could have a cup of tea and put your feet by the radiator?"

"Because I don't know if anybody's going to come fooling around again, I only think there's a chance, and there's no use having the old man lose any sleep for no reason. I let it be known around St. Ulric's school that I was looking into the business of the dead cat in the church and all the Black Mass that went with it, so maybe that'll be enough to stop the shenanigans. On the other hand, if I know boys like I think I know boys, they'll have one more go before they put the game to rest and one more go could be enough to do the old man in."

Mary tries to persuade me that I'm going out into the cold on a fool's errand, but knowing how stubborn I am when I get a thought in my head and something between my teeth, she stops arguing with me, goes out to the kitchen, and makes up a Thermos of hot chocolate for me to take along with me.

"As long as you're going to go tramping around all night in the dark, you might as well take Alfie with you so he can have a walk. It'll save me taking him out while you're gone."

Alfie's all for that until we get downstairs and he sticks his nose out the door. Then he backs up and looks at me as though questioning my sanity.

"Not you too," I says, picking him up and putting him in the car.

I get behind the wheel and turn the key. It starts right up, which if it didn't I would've chucked the whole adventure for the night and gone back upstairs, which was what I'd've liked to do the minute my nose hit the outdoors too.

So I drive over to St. Pat's feeling sillier and sillier by the minute. I tell myself I got to learn not to let some vague notion get fixed in my head so there's nothing for it but to run it down like I was some crazy junkyard dog, which is what people call me behind my back—and sometimes in front of my face.

It don't take long to get over to the Fourteenth and St. Pat's what with all the sane people in Chicago home in bed and no traffic on the road.

I park the car across the street from Father Mulrooney's house. There's a dim light in the oval window, which I know is on the stair landing, and a light on behind the shades and curtains covering the windows in one of the rooms upstairs, I don't know which one.

It got pretty warm in the car on the drive over but it don't take long for it to start cooling off and then getting cold. Besides, I know I got to go out in it because if anybody's going to be on the midnight prowl, it's going to be around the back.

"You got a choice, Alfie," I says. "You can stay here out of the wind or you can come with me."

He wiggles a little and gives a little whine, which means he ain't got no choice. His kidneys has made the choice for him. So we get out of the car and we walk across the street, Alfie pausing to lift his leg against the first tree he comes to.

I go down the alley between the priest's house and St. Pat's. Alfie comes trotting after me.

There's a cold moon, just about half, floating up in a sky shaped like a bowl with the city shine all around the edges close to the earth and the blackest black—like black ice—directly over the cemetery. I lean up against the iron fence in the shadow of an old oak. The wind kicks up and my feet start turning numb.

Alfie has another pee and that reminds me I got to relieve myself as well. While I'm watering the roots of the tree and the bottom of the fence, I hear a door open. I don't know where it's coming from because there's no light coming out of anywhere at ground level. I try to stop what I'm doing but it ain't easy to do in midstream. A flashlight blinks on and off right in my eyes from over by the church.

Alfie starts barking.

Whoever it is with the flashlight starts running. I get zipped up and start running after him. He breaks out of the backyard onto the sidewalk under a streetlamp. He's got a good head start on me and I only catch a quick look but I can see whoever it is has got a big brown paper bag under his arm.

I break out of the yard just about the time he's turning the corner and go chasing after him, Alfie running just a little ahead of me, not barking any-more because he's smart enough not to waste his strength. The guy up ahead is stretching out.

I think I'm going to lose him when he cuts off the street down an alley. I'm breathing so fast the wind ain't got time to get warm and it's cutting my lungs. Then I get my second wind and I go floating up on top of a rush of them hormones or whatever which long-distance runners say gives them a terrific high. I think maybe Alfie gets a rush too, because all of a sudden he's right on this gamoosh's heels and grabs the cuff of his pants.

Next thing I know I've got the collar of the man's coat in my fist and I start putting on the brakes.

He stops and turns around, having no place to go since he's run hisself into a blind alley, throwing his arms out to his sides to show me that he is without weapons. He is also without the brown paper bag and whatever was in it.

"You don't have to choke me to death," Phil the Junkman says.

Alfie's still worrying the leg of his pants.

"And tell your vicious animal to stop tearing the

pants to my best suit, which cost me seventy-nine ninety-five off the rack plus alterations."

"Where's the brown paper bag you was carrying?" I asks.

"My God, it's you, Mr. Flannery," he says. "I thought you was a mugger."

"What would a mugger be doing out this late on a night like this?"

"Looking for honest citizens like you and me," he says.

"I know what brings me out. What brings you out?"

"I was in St. Pat's during the evening, praying for understanding and all. I must've fell asleep, it's so quiet and peaceful in there. The next thing I know it's almost midnight and I haven't even had my supper yet."

"You mean nobody saw you when they locked up for the night?"

"Well, I suppose I must've slipped down on the pew when I started to doze."

He looks at his empty hands and then at his feet as though he expects to see the paper bag there. "My supper was in that bag, which I picked up at the market before going into the church to pray."

"Is that so? Well, where is it?"

"It flew out of my hands as I rounded the corner, and for all I know it could be laying there in the gutter even as we speak."

"So let's go back and have a look."

We retrace our steps but there's no brown paper bag in the street, the gutter, or on the sidewalk.

"A bunch of cats or a beast like the one you've got there could've come along and carried it off," he says.

"Or it could be in any one of the ash cans or dumpsters we passed along the way," I says.

"Well, if you think I stashed it on the run, we can just go picking through the garbage together until you're satisfied."

I can't do that and he knows it, so he's got me stymied.

"I'll have to take your word about it for the minute," I says.

"Well, okay, then I'll be on my way home."

"Let me drive you."

"That's all right, I can walk. It's only just a few blocks from here."

"I insist. You're probably as wore out as me. Since I give you such a scare, the least I can do is see you home safe."

He don't argue anymore. We walk back to my car and I drive him to this apartment house about seven blocks away. It looks like he's got a key to the door to the vestibule because he goes right in the outside one and the inside one, too, in the time it'd take him to turn a key.

I sit there looking up at the windows of the apartments. After five minutes I don't see any lights go on, but he could have an apartment in the rear and I can't sit there forever now that he knows I could have an eye on him.

So I go home and get into bed.

Mary half wakes up and says, "God but your feet are cold. Did Alfie take a pee?"

"Yes, he did," I says, "and so did I."

I go to sleep like a rock falling to the bottom of a sewer.

15

 It's a couple of hours later, about three o'clock in the morning, when I get the telephone call from Mrs. Thimble.

"What is it, Mrs. Thimble?" I says. "Don't tell me somebody's playing jokes on Father Mulrooney again?"

"This is no joke, Mr. Flannery. Father Mulrooney's laying at the foot of the altar and he's dead."

"What?"

"Dead as in ready to be buried," she says pretty snappish.

"Have you called the medics?" I ask.

"They've been here five minutes."

"And the police?"

"They're pulling up outside."

"Have you called anybody else?"

"You were the third party I called. I thought you'd want to get over here, seeing as how you were looking into the matter and did no good."

"I'll be there as soon as I can get there," I says.

I get up and start getting dressed. Mary sits straight up in bed and asks me what I think I'm doing now.

"You're not thinking of going out again? Are you sick and delirious or do you have another wife stashed away somewhere across the river?"

"That was Mrs. Thimble on the phone. She says that she's found Father Mulrooney dead in front of the altar of St. Pat's."

"Jesus, Mary, and Joseph," she says.

I finish getting dressed and tell Alfie he should stay where he is by the hot-water heater. He don't give me any argument. I go out into the wind and cold thinking about what people say about a dog's life. The way I look at it, if you're Alfie, a dog's life ain't so bad.

I pump the pedal to prime the carburetor even though my old man tells me, with an automatic choke, it don't do no good. It kicks over on the third go, which is more good luck than I've had with the old car in one night in years.

It don't take me long to get to the church. Some of the lights are on in St. Ulric's.

I ain't surprised to see Mr. Perrea, Max Dove, and Katherine inside the church, along with the emergency mobile medics, some firemen who arrive first on these calls in case it's a suicide what left the gas jets on, some uniformed cops, and a couple of civilians nobody has to tell me is homicide detectives even though I never met them personally. One's white and one's black.

The white one spots me and walks over like he's going to walk right through my face.

"Who're you?" he says.

"My name's Jimmy Flannery," I says.

"I heard about you. O'Shea over from the precinct in your ward tells me you're a ghoul."

"Why would he say a thing like that?"

"He says that you always show up around dead

bodies. Sometimes you find them. He even hinted that he suspects you make them."

"Francis likes to make out he don't like me," I says.

"I don't think he's pretending, and I think I can understand how come."

"How's that?"

"You're one of them people goes around sticking your nose in, making out wise, making good cops look incompetent. Making honest cops look crooked."

"I never met a honest cop I didn't like," I says.

"Okay, smart guy, now we know where we stand."

His partner has come up to stand at his shoulder. He's got a face the color of coffee, heavy on the cream.

"Don't mind Shimmy," he says. "His bite's worse than his bark." He sticks out a paw as big as a grizzly's. "My name's Washington Duprez. Everybody calls me Wash. My partner's name is Hyman Shimansky. Everybody calls him Shimmy."

"Like I wish I could do it like my sister Kate?" I says.

"God, you're a smart aleck," Shimansky says.

I'm thinking that all across America police captains are pairing up homicide detectives saying, "You be the good guy and you be the bad guy. Here's your scripts, learn your lines."

"I'm a friend of Father Mulrooney's," I says. "I used to sing in the choir here in St. Pat's."

"Did you, now?" Shimansky says, putting on a fake Irish brogue.

I hope I'm not dealing here with a Jew what hates Catholics. "Well, if every friend of Father Mulrooney's came pouring through the door we wouldn't have the room to walk around, now, would we?"

I don't like to use what little political muscle I
got, but when somebody comes on strong like
Shimansky's doing right now, and I ain't got the
time or the inclination to play his game, I do what I
got to do.

"I could make a call," I says.

"You hear that, Wash?" Shimansky says. "This
son of a bitch is trying to threaten us."

"I'm not threatening, Wash," I says. "I'm telling
you. I was asked to come here by Mrs. Thimble,
and since Father Mulrooney's got no next of kin as
far as I know, I guess that makes her the one to say
who she wants to come and help her in her hour of
need."

"Sergeant," somebody calls from down around
the main altar.

Shimansky walks away.

"Don't mind Shimmy," Duprez says. "He was a
friend of Father Mulrooney's too and he's trying to
cover up his feelings."

So here we got tender-natured Jews like we got
tender-natured Irish, all blustering around acting
tough so they shouldn't break down and cry.

"Come on down with me," Duprez says. "You're
not going to like what you see."

"Who found him?"

"The housekeeper."

"Where's she now?"

"Back in the house. There's no reason for her to
be in here."

We reach the body and Duprez's right. I don't
like it at all.

Father Mulrooney's laying sprawled on his back
all over the marble steps between the presbytery
and the altar, one leg stuck straight out, the other
bent at a funny angle. The back of his head is

laying on the edge of a step, shoving it forward so his chin is pressed into his chest, and his eyes is open staring down the nave. His feet are touching one point of a big five-pointed star traced on the floor in what looks like watery blood.

"Pentagram," Harold Boardman, the young medical examiner from Forensics, says.

"Was it made with Father Mulrooney's blood?"

"The back of his head is crushed but not enough to produce enough blood to make that."

"Somebody hit him with a blunt instrument?"

"He could have died as a result of his fall or he could have been killed by a blow delivered by a blunt instrument. I won't know until I get the body on the table."

The thought of old Father Mulrooney getting cut up bothers me and I raise my eyes so I don't have to look at him staring at me like he's blaming me for not taking better care of him.

That's when I see the dead cat on the altar. It's not a pretty sight. I wouldn't swear to it, but it looks like Ignatius to me, laying there at the bottom of a cross that's been turned upside down.

"That blood come from the cat?"

"The blood in that cat's congealed. That cat was buried and dug up. Somebody's playing some funny tricks around here."

"Do me a favor, will you?"

"What's that?"

"Would you put Ignatius on the autopsy table too and tell me how he died?"

16

 I walk over to where Mr. Perrea, Max Dove, and Katherine are sitting in the back pew. They're in their nightclothes. Perrea's wearing an overcoat with a fur collar, Dove a trench coat, and Katherine a knee-length quilted anorak.

"What got you over here?" I asks.

"Mrs. Thimble telephoned," Mr. Perrea says.

"Something woke me—I don't know what—and then I heard a truck," Katherine says.

"I heard the fire engine arrive," says Dove.

"Yes, it was the fire engine," Katherine says.

"So which one of you got here first?"

"I suppose it was me," Dove says. "I walked in right after the firemen."

"How did you come? By way of the street or across the yard in back?"

"The street."

"Anybody out walking around?"

"Nothing. Except for the engine, there wasn't even any traffic."

"You came through the front of the church?"

"No, it was locked, like it always is after dark. I

went around the side through the door to St. Patrick's chapel."

"Who was next?" I says.

"I suppose I was," Mr. Perrea says. "If you're speaking, as I assume you are, of the three of us."

"That's right."

"Then it was I. At least I didn't see Mrs. Jellicoe anywhere about when I walked in through the door."

"Front door, back door, or side door?"

"Side door, the way Mr. Dove came."

"You came by way of the street, then?"

"No, I came by way of the yard."

"Through the snow?"

"That's right."

"What did you see coming through the yard?"

"See? I didn't see anything."

"Nobody in the cemetery?"

He shakes his head no.

"Did you come the back way, too, Mrs. Jellicoe?" I says.

"Yes."

"Did you see anything or anybody?"

"I saw the lights of the fire engine and the ambulance and the squad cars down the alley next to St. Pat's. I saw a few people on the street, attracted by the sirens and the lights."

"Nothing unusual? Nothing odd?"

"It was all unusual, all odd." She acts anxious, like she's willing to help but don't know what I want.

I don't know myself.

"Did anyone think to check on the boys in the dormitories when you were roused out of your sleep?"

"I did," Mrs. Jellicoe says.

"Were you on dormitory duty?"

"No, I was," Dove says. "I went in to check on them before coming over here. Katherine was already there."

"Why were you checking, Mrs. Jellicoe, if Mr. Dove was on duty?"

"Kenneth doesn't live with me in my quarters," Katherine explains. "That would make it harder for him to fit in. When I heard the fire trucks in the street, naturally I went in right away to see if my son was safe."

I look at both of them one after the other so they'd know I'm asking both of them, "And everything was all right? Nothing out of the ordinary? Everybody tucked in nice and warm?"

I think I catch a little beat of hesitation and a skittish glance from one to the other that don't quite get there because they know I'm looking, but it's not enough for me to make a case about it.

"Well, thank you for answering my questions, which you didn't have to do because I'm not a cop, just a friend of the old priest."

I excuse myself and leave by the back door, which somebody has opened by now, saying that I'm going back to Father Mulrooney's house to talk with Mrs. Thimble.

But first I cross the yard, where I see tracks in the snow, which I can't tell who they belong to, man, woman, or child, because they're all scuffed and dragged, over to the old wrought-iron gate, which looks like something out of a horror movie. The hinges is all rusted and yell like banshees when I shove against them. The gate moves even slower because there's old leaves and dirt piled up against it. Which at least tells me that nobody's used this gate lately, like when whoever done it dug up the old cat and took him into the church.

I walk along the fence to the gate that's between the cemetery and the playground of St. Ulric's. I try to swing it open but it don't budge, so at first I figure it's rusted and clogged tight, too. Then I see the chain and padlock which is keeping it closed. I stoop down and see there's no leaves blocking it in case anybody wanted to swing it open after they take off the chain and padlock. Also, when I scrunch down even more to have a closer look, I see this slick on the hinges. I touch it with my finger and it comes away with oil on it. Not old oil but fresh oil, which would let somebody open that gate without a whisper.

I go back to the churchyard gate and shove it open far enough so I can squeeze in. I kick through the old, dry leaves to the big willow which is standing there in the thin light of a false dawn spreading over Chicago like some sad old man dressed in rags looking for a place to rest his head.

There's a black hole at the roots. I can't see nothing unusual about it. It's just the empty hole where the cat was buried. I scratch around in it a little and find a stone what has been sharpened on two sides, and I put it in my pocket.

I walk from the churchyard in back, across a set of steps that go up and down through a space in a low wall that separates the backyard of the church from the backyard of the priest's house.

There's a light on in the kitchen. I go up to the door and knock. A minute later Mrs. Thimble opens the door.

I can see she's been crying, her eyes is all red, though they're dry as a bone at the moment.

"It's me, Jimmy Flannery," I says. "I couldn't find you in the church and they told me you were here."

"Oh, I'm here," she says. "But not for long. Well, come inside if you're coming in. No need to heat the outdoors."

It's so hot in the kitchen, it hits me like a wet rag in the face.

"What makes you say that?" I asks.

"You know what is redundant? Well, in a priest's house without a priest, a priest's housekeeper is redundant."

"Do you have any family, Mrs. Thimble?"

She laughs a funny laugh like a yipping pup.

"Maybe not in Chicago but back home where you come from?"

"Forty years ago?"

"Even so. Any family, any friends?"

"I don't even know if Nappannee is still standing."

"What's that?"

For a second she looks at me as though she realizes she's said something she didn't mean to say but it's too late to get it back, so she says, "Nappannee was the small town I come from."

"In Illinois?"

"No, in Indiana."

I'm so cold and the room's so hot the water in the air condenses on me. I open up my coat and flap the sides to get some ventilation or I'll drop where I'm standing.

Mrs. Thimble looks at me like I'm crazy.

"It's terrible hot in here, Mrs. Thimble."

"I didn't know how many people were going to be in and out. Sit down at the kitchen table and I'll get you a cup of tea," she says, and goes over to the stove and pours me a cup of tea that looks so strong you could tan a piece of rawhide in it.

"Well, I'm sure the diocese'll take care of you."

"Now that Father Mulrooney's dead, you don't

think it'll take them long to sweep me out the door,
do you?"

"I'm sure they'll do the decent thing."

She yips again, her eyes growing small and mean.
"Listen to you? Don't know these bishops, do you?
All they care about is money."

"The detective tells me you found him, Mrs.
Thimble."

The tears start coming. "I haven't been getting
much sleep lately, what with Father getting up at
all hours of the night and acting so strange ever
since the cat died. I thought he was getting—you
know—because of his age, and I was afraid he'd
just go wandering off and maybe get killed." She
hears what she just said and she starts wailing like
her heart'll break. "I never dreamed. I never dreamed
what he said was going on in the church was really
going on."

"So you followed him right out to the church this
morning?"

"I was dozing. Something woke me. I don't know
how long he was gone before I went looking for
him. It could've been ten minutes, it could've been
a half-hour. I don't know. Should have a night watchman. There's churches that do. But that costs money,
don't it? Father Mulrooney fought them on that
nearly all his life about money. Look what it got him."

"Well, what got him is what's going to get us all,"
I says. "I don't think the attitude of the church
about money has anything to do with Father Mulrooney
getting killed."

"Murdered? Is that what you think happened?
Was he murdered?"

"I never said murdered, Mrs. Thimble, I said
'killed.' Like he fell down and killed hisself. Don't
you think that's the way it happened?"

"How should I know?"

"Well, it's just that I've been wondering what could've happened, too. There's things that are bothering me."

"The ghost blood and the dead cat and the upside-down cross are enough to bother anyone," she says.

"I was thinking also of how the cat was buried."

"What do you mean?"

"Were you with Father Mulrooney when he buried Ignatius?"

"Yes, I was."

"Do you happen to remember did he wrap Ignatius in anything for a shroud?"

"Yes, he did."

"I thought so. I didn't think Father would bury his old friend in the cold ground with nothing between him and the dirt. Do you happen to remember what it was he used?"

"One of his old mufflers," she said. "I think that's what he used. One of his old mufflers."

17

It's still before daybreak when I go into St. Ulric's. There's a plan of the school in the lobby right by the entrance door which shows me where the classrooms and dormitories are.

I'm expecting that with thirty-seven kids boarding at the school that they're all in one big room or maybe two like an army barracks. But they got it a little nicer than that. There's two corridors, what make a cross, breaking up a wing of the building into four sections which each has a big sleeping room and a bathroom attached to it.

The names of the students sleeping in each room is on the door to each room and I find the one which has Kenneth Jellicoe's name on it, which also has the names of his buddies, Hector and Walter.

I open the door and stand just inside the room listening to them breathing. I can tell they're almost all awake but pretending they're not. There's a little night-light in a plug on the wall, not enough for me to see if any of them is looking at me but enough to count the beds.

There's twelve of them, six on a side, but only

nine of them has anybody in them. I go down the
line with my flashlight, checking the tags fixed to
the foot of each bed, until I get to Kenneth's. I feel
under the bed and find his shoes. They're still very
wet. I check that Hector is on one side of Kenneth
and Walter on the other. I pull over the chair which
is between each pair of beds and sit down, leaning
forward to look into Hector's face. His eyeballs don't
move a twitch.

"I got to tell you something, Hector," I says. "When
a person sleeps their eyeballs is never completely
still. I ain't talking REM here, I'm talking little bits
of motion, you know what I mean?"

He don't cop.

"Also a person's breathing is different. What was
you guys doing out of bed?"

Hector opens his eyes. He's looking worried. "We
heard all the fire engines and trucks. We looked out
and saw the cops' cars."

"Which is perfectly natural for anybody to do
who get's woke up during the night, so how come
you guys are all in bed pretending to be asleep
when I walk in?"

"Well, we're supposed to be asleep, aren't we?"

"Maybe you're supposed to be on your average
night, but with all this action going on over the
church it ain't natural this many kids would be
asleep through it all. Right?"

"So we blew it?"

"I'd say so. So what I'd like you to do is tell your
friends Kenneth and Walter to put on their robes
and slippers and come out into the corridors where
we could talk without the other kids here in this
room getting an earful."

"Kenneth won't—"

"I got a feeling I know what Kenneth won't want to do. But I'm telling you he better."

I get up and leave the room and go sit on a bench out in the corridor. After a couple of minutes, the three boys come out, Hector and Walter looking worried and Kenneth looking like he's ready to deny whatever I say.

"Here. You guys sit down on this bench and let me look you over," I says, standing up.

They sit down like three crows on a rail, tossing side glances at each other like they're trying to figure out what I'm going to do and maybe one of them's got a clue the other two ain't got.

Walter is rattling some marbles or something he's got in his pocket he's so nervous.

"Your shoes are wet, Kenneth," I says.

"We were out in the snow during the day."

"If you were out in the snow during the day for very long somebody would've been on you about putting your galoshes on. You were out in the snow tonight. I mean this morning."

"No, we weren't," he says.

"We can have this easy or we can have this hard. You been having a little fun playing jokes on old Father Mulrooney?"

Walter starts to cry.

I stoop down, reach out, and put my hand around his wrist. He stops rattling whatever's making the noise.

"What've you got there, Walter?" I says, trying to put the boy at ease.

He pulls his hand out of the pocket of his bathrobe and shows me five or six pieces of stone like the one I found in Ignatius' grave.

"Where'd you get those?"

"We found them in the cemetery. They're all over the place if you want to dig for them."

"All right, put them away and stop being so nervous," I says. "I'm not out to put you guys in jail or nothing like that. I just want the truth."

"We don't know what you're talking about," Kenneth says, in this voice which says that's all I'm going to get out of him and warning his buddies to clam up likewise.

"What I want to know right now is if any of you saw somebody hanging around the church when you was out."

"I wasn't outside the dorm tonight," Kenneth says.

"Me neither," says Hector, now that their leader has spoken.

"Me neither," Walter says, and that looks like it's going to be that.

All I got is wet shoes, and that's not a hell of a lot of proof of anything with snow on the ground.

"So, okay. I haven't got enough to lean on you and make you open up, but you can believe it that I'm going to get something that'll make you give this clamming up another thought."

I wave the kids into their room and then I go back to the church by the back way.

Dove, Katherine, and Mr. Perrea ain't there anymore. Neither is Shimansky or Duprez. And neither is anybody else except three men from the Mobile Forensics Lab crawling around with their tape measures, chalk, tweezers, and glassine envelopes picking up this and that, and two uniformed cops.

I go down and ask one of the cops if Boardman's still around but he tells me that the ME's gone home and that I should do the same because, as soon as the technicians are through, they're going to seal off the crime scene.

"Can I get out the front?" I asks.

"That's the way to leave," he says.

As I walk past the confessional box off the side aisle, I hear somebody whispering or taking in a breath. I pull the curtain aside a little and see Mrs. González kneeling there. She turns and looks at me, her eyes glittering from what little light gets into the box.

"Mrs. González," I says, "what are you doing here?"

"The authorities asked my husband to lock the church behind them when they go. I will do it instead because his English is so bad."

"I mean, what are you doing in the confessional?"

"I will pray for the soul of the old priest. But first I must confess my sins to God and pray for my own soul."

I let the curtain drop and leave her to her prayers.

I go out into the cold dawn. There's a rumble coming down the street a block away. I step out into the middle of the street and see these big flatbeds hauling earth-moving equipment down toward the cemetery, getting everything in place so they can start work pretty soon.

Before I go home to bed, there's one more thing I got to do. I go back to the apartment house where I dropped off Phil the Junkman. I check the mailboxes. I don't see no Phil the Junkman and I don't see no Phil Procroppolis, which is his real name, on any of them.

Somehow I ain't all that surprised.

18

 I go home and sleep for a couple of hours, then I'm up again. I go over to the archbishop's mansion to see what I can do about the old cemetery and Delvin's relatives because, for the minute, there's nothing I can do about Father Mulrooney and I might as well see what good I can do for Delvin.

His Grace Patrick Carew's not unknown to me or me to him. We've been introduced more than once and I even sit next to him once at a fund-raiser for Finny Wambaugh, who gets burned when the boiler he's tending over to St. Dominick's High School blows up and tosses him thirty feet across the basement.

His Grace compliments me at the time for the brotherly love I display in helping out a fellow Catholic even though he says rumor has it that Finny was cooking up a little poteen in a home-made still which he was heating with a steam pipe fitted to the furnace.

Anyway, it's because of this old acquaintance that I get in to see the archbishop no trouble and not much wait, even though I got no appointment.

"So, James," he says after he sits himself down in a chair like a throne and offers me the seat on the other side of his desk, which ain't quite so grand but which costs more than my living room at home. "How have you been keeping?"

"Very well, Your Grace, all things considered."

"Then it's not yourself you've come to see me about?"

"No, Your Grace."

"Is it your dear wife, Mary Ellen, then? She's a nurse, isn't she?"

I'm wondering how he even remembers I'm married let alone my Mary's a nurse. Maybe he's got a system that works even better and quicker than Wally Dunleavy's, down to Streets and Sanitation.

"It's not Mary and it's not my father, Mike, thank you for remembering, Your Grace. It's my old friend Chips Delvin I've come about."

"My old friend, too. Why didn't he come to see me himself?"

"He's getting old and forgetful, Your Grace. Or maybe he didn't want to bother you with something so unimportant."

"But important to him?"

"I'd say so."

"Then important to me. However, he wisely sent his most eloquent spokesman."

"I don't know about that. Eloquent, I mean. Or spokesman, for that matter. He don't even know I come to see you."

"Well, let's get down to it, then, shall we?" he says, getting a little impatient with all the politeness we got going back and forth.

"It's about St. Patrick's cemetery."

A frown appears between his eyebrows. I'm not the only one's been on to him about this.

"St. Patrick's has no cemetery," he says. "The old churchyard at the back was sold off two or three years ago."

"I've been wondering about that."

"Have you? And what have you been wondering?"

"How come the archdiocese sold it off. I mean it's sacred ground and—"

"No, it's not."

"Your Grace?"

"It's not sacred ground. It was desanctified in a ceremony just before the property was sold in expectation."

"In expectation of what?"

"In expectation of the removal of those buried there."

"But they wasn't removed."

"There are always delays."

"That may be, Your Grace, but if I understand you right, that means a lot of good Catholics are presently laying in ground which is no longer sanctified."

"I issued an order of interim dispensation."

"That's good," I says. "It'd make a lot of people unhappy if the trumpet blows and they find out they're not allowed into heaven on a technicality."

The archbishop don't smile. He's a worldly man and can tell a dirty joke with the best of them, but he don't think the little joke I just made is very funny.

"So, what is it you want of me, Jimmy?"

"I thought maybe you could reconsider and take back the graveyard so Mr. Delvin's people won't be disturbed and so he can be buried there if he wants to some time in the future?"

"Hardly possible."

"I don't understand that. It seems to me the

Church should be able to change its mind, if anything should be able to change its mind."

"It's not a question of changing minds. It's a
matter of realities. It was determined that the old
churchyard was of little value to the diocese, especially in light of the fact that we felt we might soon
have to close down St. Patrick's and the priest's
house. Since there was little or no protest at the
time, not even by the pastor, it was decided to
begin by selling off the cemetery, which was no
longer desirable."

"Does that mean the church is going to be sold
off too?"

"One day no doubt it will be," he says. "You
know about Father Mulrooney?"

"I was on the scene shortly after it happened."

"A terrible accident."

I just make a noise of agreement, not wanting to
tell him that I'm not so sure it was an accident. He
don't mention the possibility that a little devil-
worshiping was going on over to St. Pat's so I don't
mention it either.

"So you see," he goes on, "there's no reason for
us to try to keep St. Patrick's open in a dying
parish with a shrinking congregation."

"But you made it sound like you was already
planning to sell it off before this terrible thing
happened."

"It was on the agenda."

"Did Father Mulrooney know that?"

"He hadn't yet been told. We wanted to spare
him that knowledge until the last minute."

"In case he died in the meanwhile, just like he
done, so nobody'd have to face it?"

"You make it sound unkind. We were not being
unkind to Father Mulrooney. In fact, trying to be

kind to him was causing the diocese considerable inconvenience. We'd offered him a post as assistant pastor in another church."

"An assistant to a younger priest in another church after getting kicked out of the one he'd built and worked for all his life?"

"We all must learn when to let go. We were doing our best. Father Mulrooney refused the post. We could have considered that the end to any options we might offer him. But we let him stay on at St. Patrick's until the final decision as to its disposition was made."

"Did anybody else know about this offer of another church?"

"His housekeeper, a Mrs. Thimble, isn't it? I expect he would have told her."

"Was she going to be included in the transfer?"

"She would have gone along to join the domestic staff at the larger church and priest's house. We're not unfeeling, James."

"Except where somebody's dear departed is concerned."

"You're playing the same tune, James. It's not like you to ignore the facts and argue against the inevitable."

I wonder where he ever got that idea? But I see I'm not going to get much further sitting there, so I get up and shake his hand. He don't stand up to see me out.

"I guess you're right, Your Grace," I says. "What's done is done, and I guess I'll just have to go back and tell my old boss that his people are going to be evicted."

"Relocated, Jimmy, relocated. If the living have to move aside for progress, why not the dead? Business, after all, is business."

"That I understand, Your Grace. Like I was talking to George Lurgan, used to be the alderman in the Fourteenth, about this situation and he tells me he cut a deal with Father Mulrooney."

"I doubt that," the archbishop says, straightening up and bristling a little bit.

"I don't mean any money changed hands. I mean, there was a little quid pro quo. A little tit for tat."

"What favors were exchanged?"

"I get the feeling that George Lurgan had something that could damage Father Mulrooney or Mrs. Thimble or both in some way."

"I can assure you that we would never have countenanced any irregularity in their relationship."

"I can understand that," I says, "but what I had in mind was more like somebody in authority around here, maybe Monsignor Harrigan, wanting the deal with the oil company to go through and not wanting Father Mulrooney making any waves tells George Lurgan a little something which he can use to shut Father Mulrooney's mouth."

His face turns to stone. "I think not," he says.

"Begging your pardon, Your Grace, I don't think you can know everything that goes on around here no more than I can know everything that goes on in the Twenty-seventh, hard as I try."

So I let him off the hook and he relaxes a little bit.

"Well, it's all old news. There's some wisdom in letting sleeping dogs lie."

"Or dead cats, as the case may be," I says.

So we have a little laugh, two men of the world telling each other how they understand you got to go along to get along.

I go to the door.

"And, Jimmy," the archbishop says, "you should

do something about that cold. Blackstrap molasses and rye whiskey with some hot water. Some goose grease on a piece of red flannel for your chest, if you can find a goose."

19

I drive back over to the priest's house.

The tires sizzle along the wet roads which have been cleared of snow in a hurry, such things as the quick removal of snow being more important to the average Chicagoan than official corruption. The curbs are piled high with snowbanks already turning gray with grime. Overhead the sky's still filled with big dark clouds and it looks like there could be more snow by nightfall.

I pull up in front. Dove's shoveling out the path from the curb to the front door.

After I park the car and walk over to him, he stops shoveling and leans on the handle. He looks at my red nose and bleary eyes and says, "You should be home in bed. That's the only thing for a cold. Bed rest, chicken soup, and aspirin."

"I know I should be in bed," I says, "but there's no rest for the wicked."

"I don't think you're a wicked man, Jim," he says, giving me a grin.

"I was thinking of the people who caused Father Mulrooney's death," I says. "They're always busy,

122

so that means people like you and me got to keep busy too. Which I see you're doing."

"They're supposed to be bringing the old father's body back here to be laid out in front of the altar sometime later today or early tonight."

"That's pretty quick to do an autopsy."

"I suppose they put Father Mulrooney first in line, him being a priest and all. I guess they wanted him ready for viewing by Saturday and Sunday, when more of the neighborhood people would have the time to come and pay their respects. There'll be something for the parishioners to eat and drink in the house for those who want to stop in after they view the body, so I thought I'd clear the path and have it done."

"Mrs. Thimble's inside making preparations, then?"

"I suppose she is. I haven't seen her all day."

"She's all right?"

"Oh, yes. As right as she can be, I suppose. Katherine saw her earlier in the day. She went over to help Mrs. Thimble plan the refreshments."

"Well, I'll just go check on Mrs. Thimble myself and see if there's anything I can do for her."

I walk up the path to the porch. Since Dove started from the sidewalk and is shoveling toward the house, I have to wade through the snow, which is deeper here than it had been over in my neighborhood in the morning. So I get my feet wet again. I look down and see I'd forgot to put my galoshes on. Mary was going to give me hell when she sees my wet shoes.

I ring the bell three times with a minute in between, but still Mrs. Thimble don't come to the door.

That means I have to walk around the house to

the back door. Just as I turn the corner I hear Mrs. Thimble yelling. She's driving a cat out of the kitchen with a broom, screeching like she wants to kill it.

When she sees me, she acts sheepish.

"Hate cats," she says. "Carry fleas. Shed cat hair all over the kitchen. In the food. In my cup of tea. Will you have one?"

I says I would, even though I don't want one, because it gives me an excuse to sit down and talk to her without her thinking I was giving her the third degree. The tea's just as strong as it'd been the day before.

"Neighborhood's full of cats," she's still grumbling. "The school feeds them and they just keep on coming around."

She pours a cup of tea for herself and sits down opposite me, shoving over the sugar bowl and a pitcher with milk in it.

"Unless you'd rather have lemon?" she asks.

"Milk's fine."

She peers at me closely. "Lemon'd be better. You got a head cold and citrus helps. Vitamin C, you know?"

"I've heard," I says, pouring in some milk to cut the strength of it.

"Suit yourself," she says.

She looks like she hasn't slept much or is coming down with something herself.

"I was over to see the archbishop," I says.

"Were you?"

"He tells me St. Patrick's'll be closed."

She stares at me. "When?"

"He didn't say exactly. He also said they'd probably knock it down and sell the land."

"I knew it. I knew it when they sold the graveyard that old St. Pat's would be sold not long after."

"His Grace told me he'd made Father Mulrooney an offer of another parish."

She nodded.

"Did Father Mulrooney tell you?"

"Oh, he told me, and he also told me he wouldn't have it." Tears welled up in her eyes. "He was a stubborn old man."

"Did he say that you'd go along to the new priest's house to help out the housekeeper already there?"

She nodded again.

"How did you feel about that?"

"I was all for it, what do you think? Now that Father Mulrooney's gone and St. Patrick's'll be sold off, what do you think'll happen to me?"

"I'm sure the offer at the other church'll still be there."

"Oh, no. When Father Mulrooney refused, they put in another priest and housekeeper quick enough. There's no place for me there anymore. No place anywhere."

She was crying harder now, the tears running down her withered cheeks, her voice catching around her words.

"I'm sure the archdiocese will provide for you," I says, not believing it.

She looks at me like I'm the enemy. "Will they, now? Oh, how little you know. They'll 'look into' the matter. They'll 'seek advice.' They'll 'confer with superiors.' And, sooner or later, they'll tell me there's nothing they can do and ask me if I saved my pennies."

She puts her head down on her bony arms and weeps. I finish my tea so she won't think I don't like it, pat her on the shoulder, and let myself out.

20

Dove is just finishing up out front.

"You look distressed," he says.

"Well, I suppose I am," I says. "Mrs. Thimble's crying, and that sort of thing is always hard for me to take."

I reach for my handkerchief to blow my nose and the little sharpened stone falls out onto the flagstones.

Dove stoops down and picks it up. "That's a nice one," he says.

"Nice what?"

"Arrowhead."

"I thought it was just a piece of stone with an interesting shape."

"No, it's an arrowhead."

"I always thought arrowheads was more like this," I says, tracing a triangle in the air.

"They were more oval, like this one. This is an Indian arrowhead, all right. Potawatami lived around here."

"I've been told. Tecumseh fought hereabouts."

"Well, they call it the War of Tecumseh. He got all the Indians in the region in an uproar, but I

126

doubt Tecumseh was ever up around here, around Fort Dearborn."

"Some battles were fought here, though?"

"Oh, yes."

He hands me the arrowhead. It feels different in my hand now that I know it's a genuine Indian artifact.

"Maybe there was a battle fought right where we're standing?" I says.

"That's possible."

"Fallen warriors buried here?"

"That too," Dove says, grinning like he's enjoying the stories I'm making up in my head.

I put the arrowhead in another pocket so I won't lose it when I pull my handkerchief out to catch a sneeze or blow my nose again.

Another flatbed truck rumbles by with a bulldozer chained to it. The enemy, as old Delvin would say, is gathering its forces. It goes up to the corner, where it'll make the turn up and go up the side street and back down to the cemetery. We watch it all the way.

"Are you and Katherine having a relationship?" I says.

"Hey!"

"I know that sounds very nosy, Max, but I'm asking for a reason."

"We like each other."

"I like her, too, Max, but that don't mean I'm having a relationship with her."

"St. Ulric's has rules against teachers fraternizing socially."

"I never knew that kind of rule to stop anybody."

"It hasn't."

"How long has it been going on?"

"Six months. The relationship, I mean. We liked

each other from the start but she was still hurting very badly about her husband."

"Her son, Kenneth, know about it?"

"We've been as discreet as we know how to be. It isn't easy."

"So he might know?"

"I wouldn't bet on it one way or the other."

"How do you and Kenneth get along?"

"He's standoffish but acts like he wants to be friends sometimes. It's very hard for him, too, losing his father that way. I suppose he's looking for a male role model, someone he can look up to like he would his father, but that conflicts with his feelings of loyalty toward his dad."

"How do you feel about him?"

Dove hesitates.

"I mean, do you like the boy?"

"I'd like to do what I can for him."

"That doesn't say do you like him."

Dove hesitates even longer before he finally says, "No, I don't. I think he's devious and sly. Smart as a whip, but he'd rather spend a pound of energy getting out of doing something he doesn't like than an ounce just doing it and getting it over with."

"Like some guys in the army."

"That's right. I think he's a bit of a bully, too. I notice how he pushes Hector Carmody and Walter Click around."

"So you're protecting the boy because of Katherine."

"What's that supposed to mean?"

"When you checked the boys last night," I says, changing direction like a broken field runner, "you knew some of them had been out."

He don't say anything right away.

"Katherine knows he was out too," I says.

"I don't think they were doing any serious mischief."

"It depends on what you could call serious mischief. If what they did caused Father Mulrooney's accidental death, then I'd call that serious mischief, wouldn't you?"

"My God, you don't think they had anything to do with that?"

"They were doing something over to St. Pat's. Whether they faked the Black Mass I don't know. They'd know about such things from their religious instruction, and Kenneth's the kind would think it'd be funny to upset an old priest by playing a game on him. I'm no cop. But it's something I think the cops should know about. So unless the boys can convince me they didn't do it, I think I'll have to tell Shimansky and Duprez and let them take it from here."

Dove frowns.

"I hope that don't sound like a threat," I says. "It's just something that'll have to be done. I want you to tell Katherine what I said. I think she'll take it from you better'n from a stranger."

He nods his head and shoulders the shovel. "I'm warmed up now. I think I'll do the path around the school. You go home now and get in bed."

"I will," I says. "First chance I get."

"Before you go, what did you mean when you had a reason for asking was I having a relationship with Katherine?"

"Just that Kenneth might not like it and he could maybe figure if he caused enough trouble to get hisself kicked out of school, his mother would go with him and that'd break you and her up pretty good."

21

 By the time I get home my head feels like a balloon and my nose is running like a faucet, somebody's thrown sand in my eyes, and I swallowed some gravel. Mary's left me a note telling me she's gone over to see her mother and her Aunt Sada, that I should turn the heat on under the stew at six o'clock and take Alfie for a walk if I feel up to it. If not, I should see if Joe or Pearl Pakula, what run the grocery downstairs, will do the favor, or maybe Stanley Recore next door if he's home from school when I get home.

Alfie wants a walk very bad but it ain't in me to do him the service, so I go across the hall and knock on the door to see if Stanley's home for lunch.

When he was really little he used to beat on my door and when I went to open it he'd be running down the stairs. It took me a long time to figure it out that it was his way of telling me he liked me. The next thing after that, he used to just walk in on me, him having a way with locked doors I still ain't figured out, and almost caught me and Mary in a compromising position when we was first living together. Then he switches his affections to Mary and goes mooning around after her, being concerned for my well-being only because it would hurt Mary if anything should happen to me. When we get married he takes it like a man. Now that we got a dog, it's Alfie he seems to care about most.

He's got this funny way of talking which is starting to smooth out, which somehow makes me a little sad, because pretty soon he'll just be a moody teenager grunting and sighing like every other teenager in Chicago.

"You look awful, Jimbly," he says when he opens the door. "You gotta stock up on Vitamin C, D, and E. Also passium and wosperous." Which means I should dose myself with vitamins, potassium, and phosphorous.

"You god dime to walk Alfie?" I says.

"Oh, sure, I'll walk Alfwie," he says, giving me the eye. "You sure talk funny lately, Jimbly."

"It's da code," I says.

"Which is all right with me," he says.

I get Stanley Alfie and the leash.

"I'm going to bed," I says. "Just shove Alfie back inside da door. I'll leave it unlocked."

"You don' hafta," Stanley says. "I can get in."

"I've been meaning to ask you about that," I says, remembering the times when I'd turn around and there he'd be.

"You godda nail file?" he says.

I give him my nail file and Stanley fools around with it in the keyhole of the Yale and snaps it open. He hands me back the file and trots down the stairs with Alfie.

I fall asleep but it ain't very restful. I think I hear Stanley come in with Alfie and I think Alfie puts his nose in my hand to tell me he's back. Also the phone rings once, but by the time I swim up out of the doze I'm in it stops. It's enough to make me have to get up to take a pee.

I go into the kitchen to make myself a cup of tea. I get a tea bag because I don't want to make a whole pot. I sit there dangling the white paper bag from its string while the water's boiling. It looks like a square of cotton or gauze with dried bugs inside, not very appetizing when you come to think about it. I put it into the mug and pour in the water, watching the streamers of pinkish, then red-brown extract come seeping out. Which makes me think of the chemistry class I took with Mr. Green back when. And that's the way your brain works. Like a pinball machine. You fire the ball with the plunger and there it goes, bouncing around the bumpers, slamming into the levers which tosses it here and there, the backboard lighting up, running up the score, until bingo! you got a free game.

I remember this one demonstration Mr. Green did where he pours some water from a pitcher into three glasses half full of more water and gets three different colors. Red, green, and blue.

I go to the phone and call Max Dove over to St. Ulric's.

"You sound like hell," he says straight off.

"And feel worse than that," I says. "I want to ask you a science question."

He sounds surprised but says, "Go ahead, ask."

I tell him what I remembered.

"Reagents," he says.

"That's right. That's what my old science teacher, Mr. Green, called them. You ever show your boys a trick like that?"

"No, but I showed them how to put a mark on

your forehead with this chemical, and when you work up a sweat or wipe it with salty water, it shows up like blood. Some of those tent evangelists used to put the sign of the cross on themselves that way and get the people whispering that they were witness to a miracle of faith."

"I never heard of that," I says.

"Learn something new every day," he says.

I have my tea and then I go back to bed to think about it, only this time I really fall asleep and start to dream.

I'm in a church that looks like St. Pat's except it's made out of white marble inside and out. Father Mulrooney's saying Mass. He's wearing white vestments and even his pants and shoes are white. My father and Stanley Recore are altar boys, pouring the wine into the chalice the priest holds cupped in his hands. The stained-glass window above the altar keeps on changing color like a jukebox. Father Mulrooney's patent-leather hair is the only spot of black I can see anywhere.

I'm sitting up in the choir loft wearing my gown but there's nobody else up there with me. I'm feeling very curious about all this when Father Mulrooney tilts his head and winks at me.

All of a sudden he's wearing funeral vestments and his hair is white. In fact, his hair is now the only thing white I can see anywhere. Everything looks different. I look at my hands and they're as red as blood.

"Stop with the magic tricks!" I yell out in the dream.

I wake up with Mary's cool hand on my forehead.

"What's the matter?" I says.

"You were dreaming," she says.

"What time is it?"

"Six-thirty."

"I forgot to turn the light on under the stew."

"That's okay. You're having chicken soup. My mother made it fresh for you."

22

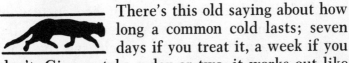 There's this old saying about how long a common cold lasts; seven days if you treat it, a week if you don't. Give or take a day or two, it works out like that every time for me and nearly everybody I know, except for Whiffy Klepitch, who drinks a fifth of rock and rye the minute he feels a sniffle coming on and gets under the covers to sweat it out. He swears he ain't had a cold that lasts more than five minutes in forty years. Also Whiffy's drunk a lot.

In spite of the truth, everybody I know has a guaranteed cure, chicken soup being perhaps the most universal one along with hot lemonade and honey. It's not good to argue with anybody who believes in chicken soup or hot lemonade with honey. My Mary believes in both. Also bed rest.

By the next morning, even getting up a half a dozen times to get rid of the chicken soup and lemonade my kidneys have had to process, I've had enough of laying in bed. I get dressed for going out right after a breakfast of chicken soup, and Mary asks me where I think I'm going.

"Well, first I'm going to talk to Harold Boardman at the morgue."

"It's Saturday."

"I'll call first, but with the amount of work they got waiting for them down there, I'd lay a bet he'll be working. Then I'm going over to St. Ulric's and see Max Dove to see if we can figure out how to search the kids' lockers without bringing a civil-rights case down around our ears. Then I'm going to look around St. Pat's one more time because something in my dream keeps coming back and I don't know exactly what it is or what it means. Then I'm—"

"You should get right back in bed instead of going out in the wet. It's warmed up some, the gutters are running with snow melt, and these are the best conditions for you to get another cold on top of the cold you already have."

"Whenever somebody dies under suspicious circumstances it's the best thing to get right on it. Every day goes by, the case gets colder until pretty soon there's nothing left to track."

"Well, you're old enough to make your own decisions," she says in a voice that says I might be old enough but, being a man, I ain't smart enough to come in out of the rain.

"Just remember," she says, "I go back on days tomorrow and I won't be able to nurse you if you have a relapse."

Then she comes over and gives me a hug and a kiss to let me know that's all the nagging she intends to do.

I call the morgue and, sure enough, Boardman's there.

"You want Alfie home?" I says to Mary as I hang up.

"If you want him with you, take him. I've got some house cleaning to do and it only bores him. Put on your sweater under your jacket."

I put on my sweater and my jacket and shove Alfie's leash in my pocket so I don't have to take my belt off and almost lose my pants in case I got to tie him up somewhere again.

"Wrap your scarf around your neck," Mary says.

"Anything you need from the grocery before I leave?" I says.

"Anything I need I'll call down and Joe'll bring it up. Put on your galoshes."

I put on my galoshes.

"Don't forget your gloves."

I put on my gloves.

Mary helps me on with my overcoat. I stand there pretending I'm a little kid so bundled up his arms stick out from his sides and he can hardly move.

"You want to give me a push to get me started?" I says.

She laughs and kisses me on the mouth before I can turn away.

"Hey, you'll get my cold," I says.

"Small price to pay."

Stanley's going out the same time I'm going out. He's wearing a new jacket.

"That's a nice leather jacket you got on there, Stanley," I says.

"It ain' ledder, it's wynl pwastic," he says.

"Well, that's the best-looking fake leather I ever seen."

It's like a spring day outside. I'm wondering what I'm doing wrapped up like an Eskimo.

"You bedder take some of dem clothes off, Jimbly, or you'll catch a worst cold," Stanley says.

But I get in the car still all bundled up out of loyalty to Mary. Alfie looks at me like I'm crazy.

By the time I get to the morgue I'm sweating, so I peel off the overcoat and leave it in the car with Alfie.

Harold Boardman's at his desk, which is in the corner of the storage room because there ain't room for it anywhere else.

There's an articulated skeleton standing in the corner which catches my eye because it seems to be looking at me.

"How much does one of them things cost?" I asks.

"One of what things?" Boardman asks.

"Them skeletons like the one that's giving me the eye."

"A real one costs maybe two thousand," he says.

"Ain't that a real one?"

"Oh, no. That's made of molded plastic. They used to come from India but they became too dear. That one costs maybe half the price."

"Pretty soon it's going to be hard to tell which is the real world and which is the imitation," I says.

"Are you turning into a philosopher, Jimmy?"

"It's the cold. It makes me moody. Have you done the autopsy on Father Mulrooney?"

"You want to see him?"

"I thought you was going to send him back to St. Pat's yesterday."

"It took me longer than I expected it to. But he'll be home before noon. So, you want to see him?"

"No. The mood I'm in, it'll only make me feel worse. Can you just tell me what you found out?"

"He died from a blow to the back of the head. Maybe he fell and hit his head on the step. We can't always tell about a crushing wound like that.

I wish I could say it was a hammer or a metal bar
but I can't do that. I can't be sure."

"You saying it was an accident?"

"I'm saying I don't know."

"Somebody was playing tricks on the old man. I
think he waited up for them to pull one of their
Black Masses again and maybe chased them. And
they hit him."

"Or he slipped and fell."

"Even then, it might not exactly be a killing but
it wouldn't exactly be an accident either. While
we're talking about tricks, I wonder was there anything tricky about that blood."

"Chicken."

"Somebody killed a chicken to write with on the
floor?"

"That's right."

"You happen to have a look at Ignatius, too?" I
asks.

"I didn't forget."

"He die of old age?"

"I'm afraid not, Jimmy. Somebody slipped the
poor old cat an arsenic mickey."

I stare at him for a while. He reads my mind.

"No, Jimmy, I ran tests on the stomach contents.
That's what caused the delay. No poison. Father
Mulrooney was killed by the blow to the back of his
head."

23

When Mrs. Banjo opens the door, she looks at my nose and eyes and she says, "I told you so. You got wet feet and you got a cold."

"Is Mr. Delvin up?" I asks.

"He's up but I don't know if I should let you see him. He'll catch your cold and then I'll have to nurse him back to health and I don't know if he's got another recovery in him."

"If that was Jimmy Flannery I saw trudging up the stairs," Delvin yells from the parlor, "you send him right in here, and if you're so worried about me catching his bugs, you might bring along a little hot toddy to fend them off."

"Early in the day, isn't it?" she yells right back.

"That would depend on when a body gets out of bed, wouldn't it? Since I find it hard to sleep nowadays and usually get up before dawn, I'd say it was midday for those of us who are such early risers."

She's shaking her head at me, denying his lies about getting up at such an hour. "It's best to humor the old man," she murmurs. "Will you have a little something?"

"I don't often take a drink, Mrs. Banjo."

"That's right, I'll bring you a little something for the cold. Go right on in," she says, and goes off down the hall.

I wonder if both of them are getting hard-of-hearing.

Delvin's sitting in his favorite chair by the window with the floor lamp shining down on an old book he's got in his lap.

"Sit down and tell me how you're getting on with my little problem."

"I've been over to St. Pat's churchyard and cemetery and had a look around."

"And what have you found that might be helpful?"

He hasn't mentioned a word about Father Mulrooney and I can't believe he's so selfish and preoccupied with his own concerns that he wouldn't at least share a moment's sorrow with me about the old priest's death.

"Have you heard that Father Mulrooney's dead?" I asks.

"Have you a poor memory, Jimmy? Don't you remember you told me about the cat and I told you to light a candle for me in its memory and I'd pay you for it when I had some change? Or are you reminding me that I owe you half a dollar?" He starts making a big to-do about shifting his hip and going into his pocket scrabbling for the money. The book falls off his lap.

I wave the money away with one hand and pick up the book with the other. I glance down at the cover. It's old green cloth imprinted with fancy gold letters, a testimonial book for some long-ago political fund-raising fair or picnic held back in 1948.

"Haven't you read the papers?" I asks, putting

the book on my knees. "Don't you watch the television or listen to the radio?"

"Every once in a while. But, actually, I don't bother much anymore. It's nothing but bad news, isn't it? What's the matter? What are you nattering on about with your eyes bugged out and your mouth open for the flies?"

"Father Mulrooney's dead."

"How dead?"

"There's only one way I know."

"I mean, did the dear man have a heart attack or what?" he asks, putting a hand on his chest.

"He had a fall."

"Mrs. Banjo!" he bellows out. "Mrs. Banjo!"

She comes walking in with a tray with two steaming glasses of her toddy in little wicker baskets so they shouldn't burn our hands.

"What are you bellowing at?" she says, loud enough to rattle the chandelier in the corner. "You think I'm going deaf like you?"

"Why is it I don't get the news from you, who gets all the gossip in Chicago and the suburbs?"

"What gossip is that?"

"No gossip, Mrs. Banjo. It's a fact that Father Mulrooney's dead."

"Oh, dear," she says.

"Did you know about it?"

"I did."

"And didn't tell me?"

She stands there, staring at him, the tears welling up in her eyes and I can see she was—foolishly maybe—trying to spare the old man she'd taken care of for so long from the sad news of yet another friend having passed on.

"Why didn't you tell me?" he says.

"I would have done."

"After the man was buried without me being there to see him off?"

I can see he's really less concerned about that than he is about the fact the news never got to him. He lost his alderman's seat, the Democratic machine he knew and loved is being junked, and not getting the news could mean he's ready for the dustbin.

"I didn't think it was such a good idea for you to be going out in this weather as I knew you would if I told you."

She hurries out of the room before he can scold her anymore.

"Damn fool woman," he grumbles, but I think he knows that she was doing what she could to spare him and keep him safe. "Where's the old priest to be laid out?"

"In front of the altar at St. Pat's. He should be there tonight and tomorrow."

"And where do you think he'll be buried? In the floor of the church?"

"I don't think they've done that in many years," I says.

"Probably not. In the old cemetery, then?"

"I doubt it. I'm sure they have a special place for priests and nuns."

"Father Mulrooney's special place should be the place he built and tended all his life." He points to the book in my lap. "There's a picture of him in that old book."

I open it and start to leaf through.

"Page sixty-two," he says, showing the remarkable memory for detail that old people often have.

There's a picture of ten or twelve people gathered around a picnic table under a sunny sky. I spot Delvin when he was forty years younger, a good-looking bull of a man, laughing like they'd caught him in the middle of a joke. Father Mulrooney, black hair plastered down and parted in the middle, blue eyes twinkling even in a face no bigger than a fingernail. Right behind him, standing back as though she don't believe she should be in the picture with these important people, is a pretty young woman.

"Who's the pretty girl?" I asks.

Delvin leans forward to have a look at where my finger's pointing on the page. "Betty Thimble," he says.

"Mrs. Thimble? Father Mulrooney's housekeeper?"

"How many women by the name of Thimble you think there could be in this city? I'll bet there's fewer Thimbles even than there are Banjos."

"What surprises me is my old man told me she was plain when she was a young woman, and she don't look plain to me."

"Your old man was in love with your mother."

"Well, the thing is Mrs. Thimble even looks a little like my mother—God rest her—looks in some old pictures I got when she was about the age Mrs. Thimble is here."

"Fashions change, Jimmy. I don't think it much matters."

"You're right, it don't."

"What matters now—more than ever, maybe— is stopping them from tearing up old St. Pat's cemetery."

"You say your great-grandmother Wilda's buried there?"

"She is."

"Was she your great-grandmother on your mother's side or your father's side?"

"My father's side."

"How far back was it that his people came from Ireland?"

"Are you asking did great-grandmother Wilda emigrate?"

He's a canny old man who's been around politics so long that he can smell it when somebody starts pumping him with leading questions asked to set up a false assumption so in case he has to appear before a court of law he can swear to whatever it is with a clear conscience. It may seem funny how people will do that—swear to a lie as long as the lie's never been spoken—when they won't actually lie on the stand after being sworn in, but it happens just about every day.

I nod my head.

"It was my great-grandfather that came from Ireland. Wilda's family was right from around here, back as far as anybody cares to remember."

I take the little arrowhead from my pocket and run it over and over in my fingers.

"Do you suppose Great-grandmother Wilda could've been an Indian?"

"What kind of Indian?"

"A Potawatami maybe?"

He reaches out and takes the arrowhead from me. "A pota*what*ami?"

"That's a genuine Potawatami arrowhead which I found in St. Pat's cemetery and there's many more in the ground over there."

"Indian burial ground?"

"Could be."

"And you want to know if it's possible Great-grandmother Wilda was Potawatami?"

"I'm curious."

"I never heard was she Potawatami, but I think

it could be reasonable to assume she was at least half Potawatami."

"I think that's reasonable."

"Don't want your toddy?" Delvin asks.

"No, thanks," I says, getting to my feet. "I've got to run along. I've got things to do."

"I'll just have it, then. Ward off any bugs you may've sprayed around. I don't want to come down sick before I go over to St. Pat's to see the dear father laid out before the altar."

24

 I go over to St. Ulric's. I take off my jacket, which has got my gloves in the pocket, and also my scarf. It's warm enough I could leave Alfie in the car, but there was something about the way Mr. Perrea looks down his nose at my pal which makes me want to annoy him just a little. So I put Alfie's leash on him and walk him across the grass toward the administration office.

Some of the boys are in short pants and very few are wearing their jackets or their caps. I think about what it'd be like to be a kid again on a day like this.

The same young woman, whose name is Arlene, is at her desk on the other side of the counter and she gives us a big smile when we come through the door.

"Hello, Mr. Flannery," she says. "Hello, Alfie."

"Is Mr. Perrea in his office, Arlene?" I says.

"Yes, sir."

"Would you ask him could I see him?"

She buzzes through and tells Mr. Perrea I'm outside and I hear him say, "Have him come in," over the intercom on her desk.

147

I tie up Alfie like I did before. I'm still squatting by the chair leg when his door opens and he's standing there.

"Have you brought Alfie along?" he says.

He comes over and pats Alfie on the head. Alfie don't even look suspicious at this show of friendliness, being the kind of dog will take what kindness he can get because I think he's lived a hard life up to the time when I saved him from execution over to the pound.

"No need to tie him out here by himself," Perrea says. "Bring him into my office."

I untie Alfie and even take him off the leash. He trots into Perrea's office and lays down next to my chair when I sit down.

Mr. Perrea looks like a different man. He's wearing a flannel shirt with the sleeves rolled up and a sleeveless sweater over it, corduroy pants, and suede desert boots. His desk is a mess of papers and a pipe is laying in a metal ashtray sending up a little smoke. I get it right there. He's not in his school administrator's mode—like they say—he's in his writer's mode. And everybody knows that writers like shambles, dogs, and odd characters like me.

"You working on your book?" I asks.

"Putting together the outline."

"*The Cat Cried Again?*"

"*The Cat Cried Twice*," he says.

"I like that better."

"So do I. How can we help you in your investigation, Mr. Flannery?"

"Investigation?"

"I've asked around about you, Mr. Flannery, and I find out you've got a nose for crime."

Which makes me realize I got to blow it, which I do.

"Chamomile tea and a peppermint inhalation," he says.

"What?"

"Clear up a cold when nothing else will. Are you helping the police unofficially?"

"Don't let them hear you say that."

He puts his finger alongside his nose and winks, letting me know that he understands the workings of such casual arrangements. I can tell he expects to get a little inside stuff from me for his research on the mystery he's writing.

I figure, what the hell, I might as well go along with it if it buys me a little cooperation, so I put my finger alongside my nose and wink right back.

"We got reason to believe this whole tragedy's been caused by schoolboy pranks," I says.

"St. Ulric boys?" He straightens up in his chair and bangs the pipe, which has gone out, in the ashtray. After which he puts it in his desk drawer out of sight.

"If it all starts as a schoolboy prank, like I think it did, I don't know why we got to look anywhere else when we got a whole school full of schoolboys right next to the church."

"A serious affair like the death of a priest is scarcely a schoolboy prank."

"I said it started as one. What happened was probably an accident."

He jumps on "probably" like he's a cat and it's a mouse. "Probably?" he says, his eyebrows going up while he starts rolling down his sleeves.

I get the feeling he's falling out of his easygoing writer's mode.

I wave my hand like it was just a way of speaking, of keeping all options open.

"The medical examiner thinks Father Mulrooney

slipped and hit his head on the marble step in front of the altar."

He settles back.

"But the cat was poisoned," I says.

He finishes buttoning his cuffs and takes a tie out of another drawer. He's definitely going to be the school administrator.

"So, how you can help is I'd like to have a look in all the student lockers."

"Seeking what?"

"Looking for something that could have strychnine in it. Like some chemical which'd be red when it was wet and disappears when it's dry. Like I don't know what else."

"We couldn't allow it. We employ the honor system at St. Ulric's. It would be a major failure of trust if we searched the boys' personal belongings without permission from them or from their parents."

"I could ask for help from the police," I says, letting his belief that I got pull with the authorities work for me.

"If they come with a search warrant, that will be acceptable to me."

"It'd be easier if I didn't have to ask the favor."

"Easier for you but not easier for me," he says, smiling like there's frost on his mustache. The Mr. Perrea I know and don't like very much is back.

He stands up and puts on the jacket he has draped over the back of his chair.

"So, if there's nothing else . . ."

I get up and Alfie gets up too, grunting a little like he does.

"And, Mr. Flannery," Mr. Perrea says, "if you have occasion to call on me again, I really do wish you'd leave your animal at home."

I wave good-bye to Arlene and go walking through

the school toward the back doors and the parking lot where I left the car. Alfie's trotting alongside me.

All of a sudden he stops and starts sniffing at one of the lockers that lines the hallway.

"You smell some kid's candy?" I says.

He gives me a look and starts scratching at the metal door.

I go over and have a look at the name on it, Kenneth Jellicoe. The lock is not a padlock but a simple one built right into the door, which opens with a key. I take out my nail file and stick it into the keyhole just to see if what I learned from Stanley really works.

It does. The door opens up as slick as a whistle. But I ain't ready to go into the business because the locks on these school lockers ain't even as good as Yales.

The inside's stuffed with all the things any school kid needs and a lot of junk any school kid wants. A sweater on the hook, a pair of galoshes, some old athletic socks, some text and note books. There's a small bag of candy bars, some girlie magazines on the top shelf, and a big paper bag laying on the bottom of the locker.

Inside the bag is a bunch of rags. I undo the rags and take out a book. It's a book of magic.

Then I shake out a big rag that ain't a rag. It's a big piece of some lightweight material like nylon or silk. It's got a black cross painted on it. In the gloom of the church who'd know it wasn't solid if they saw it hanging over the altar just right. Alfie's looking up and grinning at me like he knows he did something good.

There's no cat I can see, but when it comes to

magic, how do I know I'm not looking right at it and don't know it?

If this is the cross Father Mulrooney saw and if Kenneth worked the cat and the bloody pentagram too, it still don't explain the cross made of wood and the corpse of Ignatius, a real cat, which I saw with my own eyes.

I tell Alfie I'll buy him a piece of candy, which I figure is why he scratched at the locker in the first place.

25

I put everything back in the paper bag and take it along with me.

Then I go over to St. Pat's. The front door is locked but there's a sign that says the church will be open so the parishioners can pay their respects to Father Mulrooney starting at six that evening.

I go around to the side and that door's open but nobody's inside, so I take Alfie in with me.

He seems to know it's a special place, not that he's not the soul of dignity practically all the time and anywhere he might happen to find hisself.

There's a casket on a catafalque placed in front of the altar.

I stop in front of the altar and genuflect. It's like automatic. I don't really believe in the whole formal religious thing much anymore, but it's a custom of the place I'm about to spend some time in and it's only polite to show a decent amount of respect. Like I always put on a yarmulke if I go into a shul or attend a bar mitzvah or whatever.

Also, Father Mulrooney would say, the fruit don't fall far from the tree and my mother—God rest her

153

soul—was a good Catholic. Besides, it makes me feel like a kid again and a person could always use a little of that sort of innocence.

I go up and kneel on the prayer stool and look into Father Mulrooney's face. His nose looks very thin and his mouth looks pinched. His eyes is closed and I know that even if they was opened there'd be nobody there. There's nothing wise or jolly about him like I remember him. It's not Father Mulrooney but something that looks a little bit like Father Mulrooney but not enough to make me care. I'm going to have to call up some memories to do that.

I go sit in one of the pews. It's very quiet except for the sound of the old church breathing. The cold light of the winter day is warmed by the colored glass in the stained-glass window over the altar which shows Christ with His arms outstretched blessing the people. That part of it I always liked. The idea that there's somebody watching over us and giving us the nod even when we do dumb things. On the other hand, I ain't got a lot of charity or much patience for people who deliberately go out and do another person an injury.

I sit there thinking about the good talks I had in the past with Father Mulrooney and the first thing I know I'm thinking about what I know about his death and what I don't know about it, what I think could have happened and what I ain't got a clue about could have happened.

I got a pretty good idea who pulled that trick with the cat screaming and the shadow on the wall, but I don't think Kenneth or any of the other boys actually poisoned the cat.

Kenneth and his pals could've arranged that first Black Mass with the cross and the fadeaway blood and the cat—or whatever it was that looked like a cat that Father Mulrooney saw—but I don't think they arranged the second one because there was something more serious than they could've handled about digging up the cat and spilling chicken blood around.

The night Father Mulrooney died, Mr. Perrea, Max Dove, and Katherine from next door all went over to the church at different times and different ways. Nobody saw anything or anyone that couldn't be explained. So, if there was a third party involved in Father Mulrooney's death, there was no evidence of it.

Even though the church was kept locked against thieves and vandals there could be any number of people who could get in.

I'd have a lot more trouble breaking into a church than I had breaking into a kid's locker, but somebody like Phil the Junkman might be better at it.

I'd really like to know what made old Ignatius get up from his place by the warm electric fire and go running and wailing over to the church. Because some instinct or sharp senses told him some stranger was in it or that some strange things were going on in it?

Though why anyone would've poisoned him on the spot for that escapes me.

I'd like to know what happened to Father Mulrooney's old muffler which he used for a shroud when he buried the cat.

I'd like to know what kind of trouble there was between the old priest and his old housekeeper. Could it be over him wanting a cat and her hating them, his keeping the house like a refrigerator to economize and her wanting it like a hothouse if she could get it?

Husbands and wives've murdered one another for less.

I don't know if it'd be any different between a priest and a housekeeper who'd lived in the same house for thirty years.

Most of all I'd like to know what was bothering me which I couldn't put my finger on but which had something to do with the dream where old St. Pat's didn't look the same one minute and just like it should look the next.

There's a whisper of footsteps from the vestry and Mrs. Thimble comes through the door with a funeral wreath on a wire stand in her arms. She's wearing her best black dress with white lace collar and cuffs and black shoes with two-inch heels like I never saw her wear before. She's done her hair or had it done and it don't look like a mop. Also she don't look so dried up and skinny. For a woman her age she looks downright attractive, in fact. After seeing her picture in the old testimonial book, the possibility about the bachelor priest and the maiden lady housekeeper don't look as farfetched as it once seemed to be. They were alone in the same house for maybe thirty years. And the fact is they were only human.

She don't know I'm sitting there, and Alfie, gentleman that he is, don't even whoof when she walks in.

She arranges the flowers at the foot of the catafalque then goes to the head of the coffin and stares into Father Mulrooney's face for a long time, thinking she's all alone.

Then she goes to the altar and moves one of the candlesticks a little bit to even them up or something. While she's still got her hand on the candlestick, something catches her attention behind her

back in the church where I'm sitting and she turns
around and, looking right at me, let's go the candlestick like it was hot enough to burn her.

I know she sees me but maybe she don't know
who I am because she walks out through the door to
the vestry. I can hear her high heels tapping on the
stone floor. They sound like the footsteps of a young
woman.

26

 I'm sitting there in the silence of the church, just me and Father Mulrooney. I'm reading Kenneth's book of magic and learning plenty.

Around five o'clock González comes in through the side door. He's wearing a white shirt without a tie and the vest to a suit but no jacket. He looks at the coffin but don't go any closer to it. He walks up the side aisle, not even glancing my way, and I hear him open up the front doors in back of me.

In a few minutes there's the sound of a lot of people coming in and some shushing. A whole bunch of boys in their St. Ulric's uniforms come down the center aisle, shepherded along by Max Dove, Katherine, and Mr. Perrea, and a couple of teachers I don't know.

It's not all the kids from the school, probably just the ones who board there and whichever live within easy reach of the neighborhood who wanted to come as representatives of St. Ulric's.

They crowd up behind me until Mr. Perrea walks down and stands at the head of the coffin after kneeling for a minute on the prayer stool.

The kids walk down to the coffin two by two and file past it, bowing their heads and making the sign of the cross on themselves as they shuffle by.

Dove follows the last pair of kids as far as the pew where I'm sitting, but then he stops and slides in next to me.

"I'm not a believer," he says, like he feels he should explain or apologize.

The kids start walking back up the aisle.

I put the book of magic next to me with the pages opened.

Katherine's kneeling on the prayer stool with her auburn hair falling on each side of her face like curtains.

"Snake a hand out and get Kenneth Jellicoe for me when he comes by, will you?" I says.

Dove looks at me like I'm going to explain why, but I don't. He don't ask any questions. When Kenneth comes alongside, Dove has to reach across Hector to get his wrist. The kid looks at me and I can see he's scared.

"What is it, Mr. Dove?" he asks.

"Mr. Flannery wants to talk to you."

"Sit here until your mother can join us," I says.

"No," Kenneth says, sharp and quick, looking down at the paper bag.

"You want to talk to me alone first?"

He looks at Dove and then at me. Dove gets up and leaves us, going down the aisle a little bit to intercept Katherine when she's through praying.

"I want to know it all," I says.

"Know what?"

"I let you stonewall me before," I says, "because I didn't know enough to make you talk." I put my hand on the bag. "Now I do."

He starts to squirm.

"You tell me you're going to be sick or got to take a pee, you're going to have to do it right where you are and then we'll tell your mother why."

He looks at me with his drop-dead look.

"I'm not out to get you, Kenneth. But it's time for you to talk. I know you made the sounds of a cat crying after old Ignatius died in the church. I know you faked the shadow on the wall."

He suddenly looks a little more confident because it looks like I fired a blank right there.

"No, I didn't. That was old Father Mulrooney seeing things or something. You can see practically anything you want in shadows just like you can in clouds."

He's right there. People are forever seeing the image of the Virgin Mary which turns out to be the pattern thrown on a wall by a tree, or a picture of Jesus Christ which is only some mold growing on an old refrigerator door. So it's not so strange an old man should see the shadow of a cat thrown on a wall by some flickering candles.

"So, Father Mulrooney seeing a shadow on the wall he thought was the shadow of old Ignatius gave you the idea. You're a smart kid. You do good in science. I'll bet you do good in the history of religion too. You know all about magic tricks you can do with chemicals, how to turn water into blood. You know all about the Black Mass. At least you know how to set one up. Animal sacrifice in a sanctified church. A pentagram written in blood. A black cross turned upside down."

Having beat me on the shadow, I can see the look in Kenneth's eye that tells me he's not going to cop to nothing. He's going to stonewall me again.

"I'll bet you know about how gunpowder leaves traces in the skin of a person's hands and how

Forensics can get traces off with wax and test for nitrates. Do you know that fadeaway chemical you used to write on the floor leaves traces too? I'll bet you do. I'll bet you know how hard it is to get it off. How every time you wash your hands it shows up again. That's why you didn't wash your hands with Hector and Walter when your mother told you to wash them before she gave you any cake. I'll bet if I dragged you out in the vestibule and stuck your hands in the holy water they'd turn bloody."

He's looking down the nave to where his mother's just getting up from the prayer stool.

"I don't think you want to ask for any help from your mother," I says. "That's what you want to avoid. Her knowing about what you done."

"If I tell you about what we did and how we did it, does that mean you won't tell my mother and you won't tell Mr. Perrea either?"

"You tell me about it and we'll see. You want to make a bargain and you got nothing to bargain with."

"So, why should I make it easy for you, then?"

"Because if you can convince me you learned your lesson that it's not so smart to go around trying to scare people, I'll maybe have second thoughts about handing you over to the law."

"After Ignatius died we got the idea—"

"Hold it right there," I says. "You just start opening up and already you're leaving out some important stuff."

"What's that?"

"How Ignatius died."

"I thought it was just old age."

"So did I when I first heard about it, but it wasn't."

"How did he die, then?"

"I'd say it was something he ate. You kids ever feed old Ignatius anything?"

"That cat didn't like kids. In fact, he hated kids. I'll bet some boys must've teased him or hurt him sometime when he was little," he says piously, "and he wouldn't come near any of us."

"Before your time?" I says. "The boys at St. Ulric's wouldn't do anything like that, would they?"

"I don't know when Ignatius got to hate kids, I'm just telling you he did, that's all."

"Anybody else feed the cat on a regular basis?"

"I don't know about on a regular basis, but I saw Mr. or Mrs. González feeding him now and then."

"Anybody else?"

He hesitates and his mouth gets thin, so I know he's going to be stubborn again.

"Your mother fed him sometimes, ain't that right? Hey, it don't take a lot to figure out that somebody works in a kitchen all day would feed the church cat if she liked the cat."

"Okay."

"But you never fed the cat anything?"

"I told you. He wouldn't come near any one of us."

"Well, I meant like just dropping a nice little piece of meat or something on the ground."

He's staring at me with his mouth half-opened. Like I say, he's very smart and it's dawning on him.

"Somebody poisoned Ignatius," he says, his eyes filling up, "and you think it was me."

All of a sudden I like the kid. All of a sudden I don't see a smart aleck, I see a bright kid who lost his father and misses him something awful. He's like a small boat thrashing around in the storm of life without a rudder, which might sound fancy but which is the thought I get.

"I'd never do anything like that. I'd never kill a helpless animal."

I put my arm around his shoulders. Kenneth stiffens up for a second, then gives in to me and leans against my side.

Katherine has walked up the aisle and Dove has stepped out from the pew and stopped her from coming over to us. He's talking to her in a low murmur and she's looking at her son and me with my arm around him and a little sad smile flickers on her mouth for a minute. Then she lets Dove walk with her on up out to the vestibule.

"So, okay, Kenny, you want to tell me about it now? Was it you meowing under Father Mulrooney's window a couple of nights after he buried old Ignatius?"

"It was Walter and Hector who did that. Walter had this little tape recorder his mother and father gave him for his birthday. He was taping everything. One day he taped Ignatius wailing about something. So, after they heard the old cat was dead, they thought they'd play this joke on Father Mulrooney. They thought it was funny. I thought it was dumb."

"But it started the ball rolling, didn't it?"

"Father Mulrooney saying he saw the cat's shadow gave us the idea."

"Us?"

"Gave *me* the idea. I said playing the tape recorder under Father Mulrooney's window was dumb, so then I had to come up with something better."

"The cross and the corpse of the cat and the fadeaway blood."

"The blood was easy. I painted the pentagram on the floor with a solution of mercurous nitrate in water. After it was dry, I painted it again with a solution of phenolphthalein, one to a hundred, in a fifty-percent solution of alcohol and let it dry again.

Then right after Walter set off the tape recorder under Father Mulrooney's bedroom window and we were sure he was awake, I sprayed the floor with ammonium hydroxide, which turned it red."

"What happened to it?"

"By the time Father Mulrooney went to get Mrs. Thimble to witness what he'd seen, the pentagram was already drying and fading. By the time you came to look at it, the chemical red had faded away altogether."

"How'd you get into the church after dark?"

"We didn't have to. I set it up before the church was locked up for the night. I sprayed the floor with the ammonium with a water gun."

"How'd you do that?"

"Through the ventilator in the side of the wall by the chapel."

"A little water pistol could deliver that much?"

"Not a little pistol. A water gun. You see them advertised in the magazines all the time. They look like a rifle and they hold a lot of water you can shoot in a stream or a spray. I left the trap to the ventilator open during the day and I could poke the muzzle of the water gun right through the grill."

I'm sitting there amazed at what this kid's telling me and wondering would I ever figure it all out, magic book or no magic book.

"I had to think about the upside-down cross for a while until I figured it out."

"I found the painted cloth," I says, touching the paper bag.

"All I had to do was hang it up and, after Father Mulrooney had a look at it, pull it down with a piece of fishing line and drag it right through the ventilator grill."

"Which leaves us with the corpse of the cat Father Mulrooney says he saw."

"The cat was the hardest part of all. Finally I came up with the answer. I figured what with Father Mulrooney being old and being woke out of his sleep by his old cat wailing away, and what with the pentagram traced in blood and the black upside-down cross, Father Mulrooney would be ready to make up the rest. The sacrifice on the altar didn't have to look that much like a cat, just be the general shape of a cat. So I just soaked a piece of black tissue paper in potassium nitrate and crumpled it up in a loose ball after it was dry. If you touch a corner of it with something hot, it'll burst into fire and turn into fine ashes."

"You run a horse race," I says, remembering the novelty Carlucci'd had with his cigarette papers.

"What?"

"Nothing. I was just thinking about the things we know that we don't know we know. How'd you light it?"

"Easy. I heated up the tip of a long piece of wire with a lighter and poked it through the grill."

So there it was all laid out for me. A kid fooling around with some chemistry and magic tricks he looked up in a book.

But all I had was their story about how the first fake Black Mass was managed.

It didn't tell me a thing about the second one laid out on the main altar. That might have been inspired by Kenneth's little stunt, but it wasn't the same thing at all. It was the one that killed Father Mulrooney, accident or no accident.

27

 I call home and tell Mary I won't
be coming home for supper because
I'll be staying at the church waking Father Mulrooney.

I sit there in the middle of a pew near the back,
watching the people coming in and filing by. Old
Latino women with shawls covering their hair. A
few older Irish wearing their best black broadcloth
coats and little hats made out of black felt or lacquered straw. Their husbands with white hair and
hands all worn with work, their eyes filled with
memories of when they was young.

There are young people too. All shapes, sizes,
and colors.

Not as many mourners as Father Mulrooney
would've had once upon a time before the neighborhood changed so much. But enough to make Mrs.
Thimble, who pops back in every once in a while to
invite people over to the priest's house for refreshment, feel proud.

I hear somebody wheezing like an old elephant
and I turn my head to see Delvin on the arm of his
driver stopping at my pew. He sits down and slides

across a cheek at a time. I slide over too so he won't
have to go so far.

"You see the heavy equipment up on the road
behind here?" he asks.

"Yes, I did."

"They'll be digging up my great-grandmother's
bones first of the week unless you do something
about it."

"I'm going to see what I can do."

"I know you are, I know you are," he says, and
grips my knee with his gnarled hand, squeezing it
so hard he almost makes me say ouch, the way old
men do to prove to themselves they still got the
strength. "I wish I could help you, but I got no
favors to call in anymore."

"I don't know what favors I got where it'd do any
good either. But I think when they put the first
shovel in the ground and come up with some arrowheads, there's going to be somebody standing
there ready to protest the disturbance of the ances-
tral burial ground."

"It's something when a redskin can get more attention than an Irish-American Catholic."

"Maybe that's because they been here longer and
we all feel guilty about what we done to them."

He looks at me hard. "I done nothing to any
Indians. I don't think I even know any Indians."

"For God's sake, don't say that," I says.

"Oops," he says, "except for some of my relatives, of course."

"I went over to see George Lurgan."

"I'll bet that did a lot of good."

"He said there was no squawks from anybody
when it was sold off, so why was I blaming it on
him?"

"No squawks? How about Father Mulrooney?"

he says. "I let it slip by me but it was happening to his own churchyard and he wouldn't've let it slip by him."

"Apparently Lurgan had something to use against him. Something about Mrs. Thimble, I think."

"Oh, dear, so that was it, was it?"

"You know something I don't know maybe you should tell me. Otherwise I'm sitting in the game not knowing there's an ace missing," I says.

He blows out his breath and takes a handkerchief out of his pocket to wipe his eyes. "Some things are best forgotten and forgiven."

"You got to talk plainer than that. Are you telling me these old rumors and suspicions about something romantic going on between Father Mulrooney and Mrs. Thimble are true?"

He stares at me for a long minute, then smiles, "That would have been nice if it was so. No, nothing I know of ever passed between them of that sort. I don't know what their deepest feelings were, but back when they were young there wasn't so much of that sort of thing going on."

"There's much of that sort of thing always going on," I says.

"Maybe you're right. But I'd take an oath that Father Mulrooney was faithful to his vow of chastity, just like he was to all the others. If Mrs. Thimble had other hopes, they were never consummated. And maybe, if she loved the priest, it was enough, after all, for her just to take care of his house and bring him his slippers and have him to talk to in the evening. I don't know but what, except for young passion, marriage gets any better than that with most people."

"Are you going to tell me or ain't you going to tell me?"

"Mrs. Thimble came from a little town in Indiana."

"I know. Nappannee. She told me."

"She did, did she? I wonder why? Anyway she was a young married woman. Married to a brute of a man."

"Who was killed in the war."

"No, who was never killed in the war. You going to tell it or am I going to tell it?"

I shut up and look contrite.

"Who was killed by his young wife, Betty Thimble."

"She was a murderess?"

"Self-defense. He beat her every time he got drunk, and that was often. There's few enough places for a beaten wife to turn nowadays. There was nowhere at all but the Church back then and she'd get little enough except advice from them. It was standard for the priest or any clergyman to urge the wife to bear her torment patiently and trust in the Lord."

"Still do."

"So I've heard. Anyway she came to Chicago and to the Church, where she sought comfort, and Father Mulrooney reached out to help her as he would do. Ended up giving her the job as housekeeper because there wasn't much else she could do afraid as she'd become of the world."

"How did she kill her husband?"

"Rat poison. There's always plenty of it around on a farm."

"Arsenic."

"Yes, arsenic."

"That's how Ignatius died."

"Oh, dear," Delvin says again, in a helpless way. He's quiet for a long time and then he asks the question.

"No," I says, "she didn't poison Father Mulrooney."

"Thank God."

"But she had a hand in some of the goings-on around here and I'm going to have to find out what."

There's a little soft commotion at the back. Delvin and me turn around to see Vito Velletri, the warlord of the Twenty-fifth, coming down the aisle with his escort, one of which tips him who's sitting there. He sits down on the end and Delvin and me slide down until we're within whispering distance.

"Hello, Vito, you're looking good," Delvin says.

"You're looking good, too. I'm not so good."

"How's that, Mr. Velletri?" I asks.

"Hello, Jimmy, you're looking good."

"You, too, Mr. Velletri."

"Well, I'm not so good, thank you all the same. The mayor's talking about reapportionment again, and if they move the line two, three blocks, the Twenty-fifth goes all the way Hispanic and they vote me out next time around."

"So what's the difference, Vito?" Delvin says. "It's time for all us old horses to lay the burden down."

"How do you like it? Retirement?"

"I hate it," Delvin says with a passion. Then he chucks his chin toward the coffin at the front of the church. "But it's better than the alternative."

"So maybe you come over to my neighborhood some Saturday we play a little bocci ball."

"I'd like that," says the old elephant to the old rhinoceros.

More and more people are coming to pay their respects. In fact, it's getting to be quite a crowd.

I spot Phil the Junkman in the middle of a bunch of people. He's all bundled up so all anybody can see is his eyes and the tip of his nose, but I know it's him.

I watch him shuffle down the aisle and then line

up to file past the coffin. He takes a minute to kneel down and say a prayer, so I begin to think that maybe he really was taking the faith. But I keep an eye on him he shouldn't duck out of one of the side doors on me.

When he comes walking back up the aisle toward the main entrance, I let him go by and then I excuse myself to Velletri and Delvin and go out after him.

He's walking up the street not going fast, not going slow. I tail him, letting him have plenty of room. He goes seven blocks over to the apartment house where I dropped him off once and couldn't find him the next time. He opens the door and goes into the vestibule, then uses a key to go through the inside door.

I'm quick enough to get in behind him before the door closes and locks without him seeing or hearing me.

I see him go down the dark hallway to the back and down the stairs to the basement. So I go down there too. He walks through the basement and out the door on the other side where the super takes the garbage cans out.

I follow him into the next building and up the stairs to the third floor. He opens the door. I make the turn at the landing. I cough, looking up at him. He turns quick and sees me.

"Don't try to lock me out, Phil," I says, "or I'll kick the door in, cough in your face, and give you my cold."

"Come on in and I'll make you a hot water with cranberry juice. Best thing for a cold."

I follow him into his apartment. I can't believe what I see in it. Television sets piled up to the ceiling, some still in their boxes, radios, and VCRs, microwave ovens, cases of costume jewelry, and silver—all kinds of silver—including some candelabras and cups which ain't the kind of silver anybody has around the house. Which is church silver.

28

 "I thought you found religion," I says, "but I look around and I see you're still stealing, you're still fencing."

"That's why everything's piling up on me. The gonifs and boosters on the street still bring me goods. I tell them I don't move stolen goods anymore. They laugh and tell me they'll bust my knees I don't take their goods off their hands."

"Don't lie to me. If they was going to bust your knees and scare the money out of you, they wouldn't bother bringing you anything to buy."

"Believe me when I tell you that I don't deal with what you'd call mental giants. They got a code of ethics. Them what ain't dopers and unpredictable."

"They bring the church silver to you? I'm waiting for another fairy tale."

"Believe me, don't believe me, that silver is evidence of an act of charity on my part."

"Charity?" I almost yell at him. "I'm willing to bet the paper bag you was carrying when I chased you the other night had some of that silver in it. Now all I got to do is prove that Father Mulrooney caught you taking it and you killed him."

His eyes grow so round with fear I'm afraid for a minute they're going to fall out on his cheeks.

"Fachrissake don't say things like that, Mr. Flannery. Whatever I done in my life, I never killed anybody and never would. I mean, why would I have to kill an old man can hardly walk when I can run the hell out of there—"

"Like you did. Like you did."

"—and leave him in the dust. Oh, no. I didn't come running out of that church, Mr. Flannery. I came walking out until you came chasing after me, scared the hell out of me; I thought you was a gonif, you was a mugger, was going to rob me and maybe hurt me bad."

I got to admit to myself that I can't see Phil the Junkman raising his hand to anyone either. That ain't his style. But I don't let him know that. I let him think he could be a killer just so he won't hold out on me about anything else.

"Be that as it may," I says, using Hilda Moskowitz's line, which makes it sound like you already thought the thing out and come to your conclusion, "you wasn't in that church so late because you fell asleep while you was praying. That's a lie, and if you'd tell a lie about that, you'd tell a lie about murdering Father Mulrooney."

It takes him a minute to clear some cartons of new electric shavers off a chair before he can collapse in it.

"Don't talk like that, Mr. Flannery, please. Even if I was the type could ever kill a human being, I could never do it to Father Mulrooney. He was bringing me back to the straight and narrow. He was helping me back to God. I loved the man."

"So just tell me something I can believe."

"Mrs. Thimble," Phil the Junkman says.

"Mrs. Thimble what? You saw Mrs. Thimble kill Father Mulrooney?"

"My God, no. I was in the church that hour of the night because Mrs. Thimble and me had an arrangement."

"What kind of arrangement?"

"She gives me the church silver and I goes out and sells it for her. What I can't sell because it can be traced too easy, I was going to melt down and sell for bullion."

"Mrs. Thimble was stealing from St. Pat's?" I says, hardly believing my ears.

"She didn't think it was stealing. She said it was taking what was rightly theirs, hers and Father Mulrooney's. The pension the Church wasn't going to provide. The money she was going to use to save them both from the gutter after the archbishop threw them out in the snow, an old, old man and a woman past her prime."

"How long has this been going on?"

"Six months, maybe eight. Little things at first. The candle snuffer, which she replaced with one made out of chrome I found that only cost a finnif. She complained about how they had to keep the furnace turned down or off with fall and winter coming on. So, at first all she was doing was trying to get a little extra household money nobody'd know about."

"So, when did she start talking about what might happen to them after they got thrown out into the snow?"

Phil the Junkman thinks about it, then sticks up his finger. "About three, four nights after the night I see you looking at me through the door when I was out in the hall waiting to see Father Mulrooney."

Right after Father Mulrooney saw that first Black Mass Kenneth set up to fool him.

"She got in touch with me and told me to meet her at the church late at night. She gives me those big heavy candelabra over there. When I ask her what she's going to do if anybody notices they ain't there on the altar, she tells me not to worry, she's already got a replacement pair of silverplate looks almost like the real ones. She puts the real ones in a paper bag and tells me there's going to be lots more. Everything in the church worth selling. Then she lets me out the back and you come running the hell after me."

"What was you doing coming to visit Father Mulrooney that time of night the night I was visiting too?"

"I had one of those what they call a crisis of faith. It's very hard at first when you come around and start believing in God."

29

 I don't want to go talk to Mrs. Thimble while the people are viewing Father Mulrooney and the wake's still going on. So I sit in the back of the church and watch the people keep filing in, not a lot, like I say, but plenty. More, maybe, than the old priest would've expected or hoped for.

While I'm sitting there I'm thinking about this other problem I got trying to keep the excavators what got their heavy bulldozers, back hoes, and trenchers up on the street on the other side of the cemetery, ready to go to work on Monday, day after tomorrow, ripping away without a care or a worry in the world.

I go over to St. Ulric's to the room where Kenneth, Hector, and Walter live. It's not quite yet their bedtime. They're sitting or laying on their beds. Some are sitting at their desks reading or doing homework.

Kenneth sees me and jumps off his bed. Walter leaves his desk and comes over to stand behind him. Hector I don't see.

I wave Kenneth to sit down. "I'm not here to

cause you kids any grief. I come to ask Walter for a favor."

Hector comes in the dorm with a towel slung over his shoulder. He sees me and for a minute I think he's going to run, but Kenneth gives him the sign that's everything's okay.

It looks like I've got these kids really scared and I don't like to do that to kids. I mean, they got to know what's right and wrong, but I don't think it's a good idea teaching them by scaring them half to death and threatening them with punishment you will or maybe won't deliver.

"All I wanted, Walter, was to ask you if I could have some of them arrowheads you showed me the other day."

He lets out a little whoosh of air and goes over to his locker. He comes back with a little cloth bag full of them.

"I've got some," Kenneth says.

"Me too," Hector pipes up.

They go to get me their treasures.

"I'm not going to need all of them. When you salt a mine you don't want to overdo it."

"You going to play a trick on somebody?" Kenneth asks, and I can see he's saying to himself that I think it's okay for me to play a trick after I give him hell because he played a trick.

"There's tricks and there's tricks," I says. "Some tricks is good and some not so good and some tricks are just for fun. Like it's not a very good trick to pull somebody's chair out from under them when they're going to sit down. A person could bust his spine and be crippled for life. It's not very funny putting a garden snake in somebody's bed. A person could die from a heart attack. You understand what

I mean? You got to consider the consequences every time you think about pulling a gag."

"You're going to work a con on somebody," Kenneth said, which is pretty sophisticated talk for a kid, except nowadays they get it all on the television by the time they're five.

At first I'm about to protest and try to explain the moral issues involved here, but instead, I give them a grin and says, "Let's hope it does the job."

I take some arrowheads from each kid's stash.

"I owe you a favor. All three of you."

"That's okay," Kenneth says.

"No, I owe you a favor. You got my marker. That's the way it is. Any right-thinking man always pays off his honorable debts."

I go over to the cemetery to look over the lay of the land.

They already got it surveyed and marked out with string. I been around construction in the sewers long enough to be able to read what's going to happen next, where they intend to start digging on Monday.

I take the shovel I keep in my car to dig it out if I get caught in the snow, and dig a hole right where they'll take the first scoopful. I sprinkle the hole with the arrowheads and cover it all up again. Then I do what I can with the snow that's been protected from the sun on the north side of some of the headstones to make it look like the ground ain't been disturbed. With all the tramping around that's going to happen Monday morning, I don't think anybody's going to notice.

Then I put the shovel in my car and go back into the church. About ten o'clock it's really thinning out, only one or two people coming in every ten minutes or so.

By eleven I figure it's over and that everybody who wanted to come has been there. Anybody else will come to Mass on Sunday.

It's time for me to talk to Mrs. Thimble, which I'm not looking forward to.

30

 There's somebody coming out of the front door of the priest's house when I climb the steps to the porch.

It's a street person, wrapped up in three or four sweaters and how many skirts I don't know. She'll need everything she can get to cover herself with because the weather's stopped playing summer, spring, fall, or whatever and has settled down hard on the side of winter.

She's got a wool hat smashed down over her ears and she's wiping her mouth on her sleeve. I can see her pockets is lumpy with things she's carrying. Probably some of it is food from Mrs. Thimble's table.

"You're late," she says, "but there's plenty of food. In fact, I never seen so much food." She belches and grins at me with great pleasure, living for the moment.

I go inside and stand in the hallway listening for a moment. I walk into the big old-fashioned dining room. It looks like an army's had supper there. Half-empty tuna casseroles and pots of beans, sliced-up loaves of bread, cold cuts starting to curl around the edges, and bottles of wine. Food to feed the living in their hour of sorrow for the dead. One of the most human rituals I know.

It's very quiet in the house.

There's nobody in the kitchen.

There's nobody in the big living room.

The clock is ticking on the mantel and that surprises me, like I had this idea, without knowing I had it, that since Father Mulrooney's dead the clocks in his house shouldn't be running.

I hear a little muffled cough from the study he used as a bedroom.

Mrs. Thimble's sitting in a rocking chair beside the window, looking out into the night. She's holding a muffler on her lap as though it's a cat she's petting. She turns her head to look at me and the light of the lamp on the bedside table catches her eyes and I see a young woman staring out at me from 1947.

"You know all about me, don't you?" she says.

"Not everything."

"You know how I came to be here, keeping house for a priest in Chicago?"

"I know about your husband. I know about forty years ago."

She raises her eyebrows, asking me a question.

"My boss, Mr. Delvin, told me."

"Yes, he knew."

"He wasn't giving away your secret for no reason. He wanted me to understand."

"It doesn't matter anymore," she says.

"You want to tell me what happened? How it happened?"

She shakes her head slightly. It's no more than a tremor.

"Maybe I should tell you?"

Her head don't move.

"You killed the cat."

"He was old. So old. The poor creature had feline leukemia. It had cancers and arthritis. Every time a flea bit it, the creature got infections. We couldn't keep on taking it to the animal doctor. We couldn't afford it."

"So you put Ignatius out of his misery?"

She looks at me, thinking that one over. Looking to see if there's some kind of trap in saying yes, that's what she did.

"That wasn't the only reason you killed the cat, was it?"

"He wouldn't leave St. Pat's. He wasn't going to leave St. Pat's until they drove him out into the gutter with nothing but the clothes on his back and me right behind him. Or maybe he wasn't going to leave till they carried him out feetfirst and buried him in some strange place." Her face twists up in a sudden pain and sorrow. "Just like it's happening."

"Did you think if you killed his cat that'd take the heart out of him for staying and hanging on? Did you think if he agreed to leave St. Pat's and let the archdiocese do whatever they wanted with it that they'd find another place for you and him?"

She frowns, then smooths the lines away with a hand that's like a piece of soapstone. She's trying to sort out what she was thinking at the time she did it. Trying to pick the truth out of the muddle of her feeling then and right now.

Just like the rest of us, she can't be sure what she really meant to do; how much she lied to herself that it was mercy for the cat instead of a desperate shot at doing something—anything—about the state she was trapped in with the old priest.

"So maybe you didn't have that notion when you put Ignatius to sleep. Maybe it was after the boys thought they were funny meowing under Father Mulrooney's window, getting him all upset, getting him seeing shadows on the wall that you started thinking about how Ignatius' death could be a way to make Father Mulrooney want to leave."

"Not then," she says. "It never entered my mind then."

"Okay. So, after the boys pulled the Black Mass with the upside-down cross and the tissue-paper cat that burned away to fluff and the fadeaway pentagram of blood on the floor. You must've seen them setting it up. Some part of it. You must've been in the church."

She don't say yes, she don't say no.

"Sure. You was probably behind the grill between the narthex and the nave or maybe in one of the little chapels on the other side of the church from St. Patrick's chapel. You was there meeting Phil the Junkman, handing some stuff over to him."

Her eyes widen a little and her mouth twists almost like she's smiling. She's got the kind of face which does very little but which you can read every little tic and tremor like a book.

"What could be a better place to meet than a church?" I goes on. "Anybody sees Phil the Junkman going into St. Pat's, nobody wonders what he's doing. Even thieves can go into a church to pray."

"We needed money for everyday things. A little decent meat on the table. A new suit for Father Mulrooney. Medicine for the cat."

"And what else? After you got the idea from the boys and decided to keep the ball rolling. After you decided to put on your own Black Mass that'd stand up to witnesses. Not burn away, fly away, fade-

away stuff, but what looked like the real thing.
Real blood even if it was chicken blood. The corpse
of a real cat. A cross of real wood turned upside-
down. Did you think that maybe you might as well
gather up a little nest egg, a little moving-on money?"

"The candles burn just as good in silverplate as
they do in real solid silver," she says.

We sit there for a minute saying nothing. She
sighs and it's like I know she's giving up the last of
her resistance.

"You want to tell me now what happened the
night Father Mulrooney died?" I says, so soft it's
almost like I believe she'll think it's her own mind
speaking to her.

"Philip made the cross and brought it to me. I
never told him the real reason why I wanted it. I
told him some story about a Church celebration
and he never doubted it. I'd found the silverplate
and I gave him the solid-silver candelabra to sell.
Then he left."

"I saw him leave," I says. "I chased him and he
threw the candelabra away somewhere."

"Into a storm drain. He fished them out with a
grapple after you were gone."

"So, then?"

"I prepared the altar. Afterward I felt nervous
and sick," she says. "I went into the confessional to
sit down a moment before I went back to the house
to rouse Father Mulrooney out of his bed. But he
was already up. He was a very courageous man, you
know. A man of unquestioning faith some ways. A
very cynical man in others. Superstitious one minute and skeptical the next. I should've known he'd
pretend to believe in the ghost of the cat and the
shadows and the disappearing ceremony and then
go try to find out what was really happening.

"He came into the church through the side door just as I was leaving the confessional. I'm sure he couldn't tell who it was in the gloom and shadows at the distance. He shouted to me and I crouched down and tried to get away between the pews to the doors on the other side. He started running after me." The tears are running down her face but her voice don't change one bit. "I heard him cry out and crash to the floor. When I went back and knelt beside him he—"

She can't go no further.

I tug on the muffler she's got in her lap.

"This the muffler that Father Mulrooney used to bury Ignatius?"

She nods.

"Why'd you keep it, Mrs. Thimble?"

"I made it for Patrick with my own hands."

It's the first time I ever hear her call Father Mulrooney by his first name. I wonder if that was what she called him all those years when they was mostly alone in the house.

"For his birthday," she says. "Twenty-five years ago. I thought he valued it. He said he did. Then he used it to wrap up a dead cat. I wanted it for a keepsake of that birthday twenty-five years ago when . . ." She shakes her head. "Foolish old woman."

I stand up. "Will anybody be coming around to help you clean up?"

"Oh, yes. After the funeral Mass tomorrow I'll have plenty of hands."

"I'll leave you alone now if you want me to."

"Please."

I walk to the door.

"Mr. Flannery?"

"Yes?"

"What will happen to me now? When will you tell the police what I've done?"

"I'm not telling the police anything. Father Mulrooney died by accident."

"I killed him."

"No. An accident killed him. We blame ourselves for every accident we might cause for somebody else—I don't mean driving drunk or something like that—we'd be in the confessional twenty-four hours a day. Who am I to go around judging you for what you done? Who's anybody to do that? One thing, though."

"Yes?"

"If the archdiocese does right by you. If they provide for you a decent living and a decent place to live, will you put the silver back?"

"If it'll make you feel better."

"No, Mrs. Thimble. What I was thinking is it'd make *you* feel better."

31

It's not usual for Roman Catholics to have funeral masses on a Sunday, but it's not prohibited, so it's sometimes done in special cases like with Father Mulrooney. So, it's Sunday when Mary, Mike, and me go to the high funeral Mass at St. Pat's. Charlotte and Aunt Sada come along because they heard so many stories about the priest that they would like to pay their respects to a good man who had something to do with the lives of Mike and me, the new men in their family.

The church is packed right to the doors. The people spill down the steps and into the street, which the cops've roped off.

We got places saved for us down front with Mrs. Thimble.

As we're walking through the crowd in the street and on the steps, sitting in the pews and standing in the aisles of the nave, we're saying excuse me, pardon me, to blacks, Hispanics, Orientals, and white people. Every nationality you can think of I'm ready to bet. I'm also ready to bet Aunt Sada and Charlotte ain't the only Jews there, and that there's

188

Protestants and Muslims and maybe even Hindus in the crowd of people come to say good-bye to Father Mulrooney. To a priest. To a good man, most of all.

His Grace the archbishop hisself is doing the Mass. He's standing in front of Father Mulrooney in his coffin.

In his vestments, with the book—which he don't need, since he's knows it by heart—in his fine hands, he makes a grand sight.

Father Mulrooney would've had a good laugh.

32

 It ain't easy locating a Potawatami Indian on a Sunday night in Chicago.

I finally go see Janet Canarias, who, being a minority candidate any which way you look at it, has lists of citizens broken down into race, religion, gender, sexual preference, ethnic background, and so forth. She puts me onto a man by the name of Bill Streit, also known as Wet Mouth among the Potawatami.

I find him in a tavern over in the ward on the Near North Side known as the Roaring Forty-second. He's got a kisser like the chief on the nickel and eyes you could use for stoplights.

I remember all the things I ever heard or read about drunken Indians. I figure I struck out on this one and will have to go looking elsewhere.

"Is there something about my face that troubles you?" he says in this very educated voice.

"I was just wondering why your eyes is so red."

"There would be occasions when I'd knock you to the tiles for intruding on my privacy with such

impertinence, but I'm feeling mellow tonight and
give you a reprieve."

"I didn't mean to be rude."

"I have a case of pink eye," he says. "Nothing
severe, just annoying."

"Stanley, the kid what lives across the hall from
my wife and me, had purulent conjunctivitis just a
couple of months ago."

"Do tell?"

"My wife's a nurse. Boric-acid eyewash. It'll go
away when you get over the flu. My name's Jimmy
Flannery." I stick out my hand and he takes it.

"Mine's Bill Streit."

"Also known as Wet Mouth."

"Who told you?"

"Janet Canarias."

"A fine lady. So, you thought Wet Mouth meant I
was gone to drink, isn't that right?"

"The thought crossed my mind."

"Well, it doesn't. But don't ask me why my mother
named me Wet Mouth. It could be a joke. Indians
like to play jokes. You white eyes don't know that.
You think of us as a serious people."

"I'm glad to hear you like to play jokes."

"How's that?"

I tell him about the churchyard and cemetery at
St. Pat's and how it was sold off to the oil company
which is about to build a gas station on it and how a
lot of people—including my old friend and patron
Chips Delvin—is very upset about their relatives
being evicted and how I put the arrowheads back
what had been dug up by the kids at St. Ulric's.

"So that it can be declared an archaeological site
and construction delayed?"

"Maybe delayed long enough the oil company
loses interest. Nowadays you raise enough stink

about a corporation opening a gas station, a supermarket, or a parking lot where the people don't want it and you can change their minds about building. It ain't worth the damage to their public image."

"Why should I care about a lot of white eyes?"

"I don't know if you should or you shouldn't. I'm not going to argue about that. But suppose the cemetery was on top of an old Indian burial ground? Would you care then?"

"Of course I'd care."

"What would you do about it?"

"What could I do about it?"

"Raise hell."

"Who'd listen?"

"Janet Canarias would listen. My old man, who's Irish would listen. My wife would listen. Her mother and aunt, who're Jewish, would listen. I'd listen."

"That's what you say, but I still don't know you'd really come to my assistance, do I?"

"You got to take my word."

"My people aren't buried there. That many arrowheads means it was a village, maybe a battle ground, but not a burial ground."

"I thought I'd ask," I says. "I thought I'd ask you to just be there tomorrow morning when the earth mover scrapes up the first shovelful of dirt. I thought you could spot the arrowheads and say something like, 'Hold it! You maybe are disturbing the resting place of my ancestors.' "

He's staring at me like I'm a little off my bird.

"Or words to that effect," I says, finishing up like a lame duck without a crutch.

"Who'll be around to hear those immortal words, that brave declaration?"

"Persons from the *Sun-Times* and *Tribune*. Also

from the radio and television stations. This is a news item. Will you do it?"

He thinks a minute, then he grins and says something like "*Nockamee nanoo paw oona.*"

"How's that?" I says.

"You bet your sweet ass," he says.

33

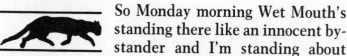 So Monday morning Wet Mouth's standing there like an innocent bystander and I'm standing about twenty yards away under the willow tree where I already put the carcass of old Ignatius before any of the workmen had arrived. I see Max Dove and Katherine standing at the back door of St. Ulric's. When they see me, they wave.

Also some suits from the oil company, wearing yellow hard hats, are standing around.

Just like I figured—especially since I made some phone calls—the media, as they say, is well represented. There's even a camera crew from one of the local stations.

The crane operator climbs aboard and kicks the engine over. It puffs like a dragon in the cold air. He pulls this lever and that lever and the monster rumbles forward right to the spot I knew from the stakes would be the corner of the excavation. The chains and gears rattle and clang. The big bucket hits the ground with a thump. The steel teeth bite into the ground. The operator jams it in, digging the teeth into the earth, then tilts and lifts the scoop.

As he pivots the arm and lifts the scoop over the waiting truck, the dirt streaming from the teeth of the dragon, Wet Mouth steps over the string marking out the site and picks up an arrowhead.

"Geddahell outta there whatchatink you're doin'!" the foreman yells.

"This is a Potawatami arrowhead," Wet Mouth yells right back, loud enough for the media to hear.

"So shove it inya pocket and gettahell outta there!"

"This is undoubtedly an Indian burial ground," Wet Mouth says.

"Howdahell you know that?" he demands.

One of the suits goes hurrying over.

"Because my name is William Streit, also known as Wet Mouth, subchief of the Potawatami."

The cameras are snapping and the television lens is zooming in close.

With all this attention, Wet Mouth gets carried away. He opens up his overcoat and, holding it out from his sides with outstretched arms, steps in front of the earth mover.

"Do nothing more!" he shouts. "I will defend the sacred bones of my people to the death if I must!"

34

This was pretty good stuff.

By noon there was a gathering of Potawatamis, some in tribal dress.

Wet Mouth had gone home to get into his own elkskins and feathers.

More important suits have hurried in from corporation headquarters to see what the hell was going on.

St. Ulric's has declared a half-holiday, partially in honor of Father Mulrooney and partially so the boys could witness civil protest in action.

My father arrives escorting Mary, Charlotte, and Aunt Sada.

Janet Canarias appears with several of her aides and half a dozen aldermen and their aides in tow.

Alderman Moskowitz arrives with her crowd from the Fourteenth.

Patrick Carew, His Grace, the archbishop, arrives in his black limousine. With him is his financial shark, Monsignor Harrigan. When he spots me he comes rushing over like he's going to commit mayhem.

"I might have known you'd be into this somehow, Flannery."

"I don't know what you have in mind, Monsignor. I was over to see if Mrs. Thimble—poor old woman who's beside herself with fear that, now that Father Mulrooney's gone to heaven, she'll be thrown out into the snow and cold—was in need of some comfort, seeing as how the Church authorities have no time for such matters as human compassion."

"You're a liar," he says.

"If a man without a collar was to call me out like you just done, I'd be quick enough to oblige him," I says. "But, in the circumstances, even if you can't give me the benefit of the doubt, the least you could do is find a little charity in your heart for a poor sinner."

He grabs my elbow and says, "Come along and tell your story to the archbishop."

Since I see the mayor and his men has arrived and are joining His Grace, even as we're speaking, I don't make a thing about him manhandling me the way he's doing but go along as meek as a lamb.

"There's a little something going on here that somebody's going to have to explain," the mayor says.

I start giving him a song-and-dance, filling him in on the history of how the Church disposed of the cemetery full of good Catholics—so, okay, in this day and age who expects piety and respect—but now it's turned into something more serious.

Now they want to defile what could be the sacred burial grounds of the Potawatami and the mayor should know how upset people get about kicking around helpless American Indians. Unless of course, it's something like stealing their water rights or taking back pieces of their reservations because minerals have been found underground.

I see Delvin's old black sedan pull up at the curb.

Delvin gets out of the back. It takes a little doing because he's not only dressed in deerskins with fringe all along the sides of his legs and arms but he's got a huge war bonnet on his head and hanging down his back almost to his moccasins.

"This time it ain't going to be so easy pussyfooting around it," I goes on. "The white eyes ain't going to abuse the red man this time because a very important person with *them* is a very important person with *us.*"

I lifts my arm and points my finger.

"There's the man who walks in both worlds," I says, finishing on a high note.

Delvin looks grand, I must say, except I should tell him the war paint is a little much.

The mayor looks like he's going to raise hell or bust out laughing.

Finally he says, in this choked voice, "What can I say, Flannery? You win."

Well, I don't exactly win, but what I says to Monsignor Harrigan gives him a notion about what I might do if aroused, so he makes sure Mrs. Thimble gets a pension, and the mayor calls for an investigation of the burial site.

By the time they find out no Indians were buried there, the oil company decides all the publicity's doing them no good at all. So they give up the idea of building a gas station behind St. Pat's and deed the land back to the archdiocese—which pleases Monsignor Harrigan, because he's a man what likes something for nothing.

The nicest thing of all is that Father Mulrooney,

whose body was kept at the mortuary in a vault, can be buried there.

Right by the willow. His head is pointing toward St. Pat's, and the grave of Ignatius, his old cat, is at his feet.